THE SPIRIT OF COFFEE

Elle Hyde

PublishAmerica
Baltimore

Softcover 9781462694822
PUBLISHED BY PUBLISHAMERICA, LLLP
www.publishamerica.com
Baltimore

Printed in the United States of America

PROLOGUE

As Joe Bauchmann walked back to the house from the barn, a cold rain fell from the ominous clouds overhead. The frozen drops of rain pounded his body as he limped over the rough terrain of the barren pasture. He did not feel the chill nor did not feel the pain of his arthritic joints as his knees absorbed the shock of each step. All Joe could feel were the overwhelming pangs of guilt welling up within his stomach. Joe was the head of the Bauchmann household, a struggling farm family consisting of himself, Melinda and their three children, Peter, Bonnie and Noah.

Joe reached the kitchen door and viewed Melinda through the window, sitting at the kitchen table. Her hands rested on top of the table while she twirled a soggy handkerchief around her fingers. He did not hesitate to speak. He started the speech that he had been rehearsing over and over in his mind.

"The horse will not be a runner. Doc Fonder said the injury will keep him from runnin'." Joe did not wait for her response, he continued without hesitation.

"I spent the money meant for cows on that horse."

There was no response from Melinda. The silence was awkward and rendered Joe even more insecure, so he continued to speak.

"Melinda, I took a chance, for you, for us. The horse won't run and I can't get the money back…" He looked into her eyes trying to evoke a response from her. Melinda sat quietly without comment.

"We will just have to bear the winter and wait until the spring for me to make it up. I am sorry Melinda. I thought I was doin' what was right?" He finished his speech with this final word.

Melinda could not stay silent any longer. "Bear the winter, with what? That is all you have to say to me Joe Bauchmann? For once in your life, be honest with me and with yourself."

Joe did not know how to answer her, so he didn't.

"For heaven and mercy's sake. You! You wanted the horse. They were your dreams of more. Not for me, or for our kids. Your father, rest his soul (she crossed her chest), told me your head was not grounded and your feet not on solid ground. He told me you were lazy and wanted a short path in life. I stood by you and where am I?" Melinda continued chastising Joe.

"You lied to me. You placed us in a hardship for this upcoming winter. You didn't do this for me Joe, it was for you. You can't accept that you are a struggling farmer. You will always be a struggling farmer and no more. Blame one man, yourself." Melinda spoke firmly looking directly into his eyes.

Joe felt the pain of the last comment strike his abdomen like an unexpected punch. He turned and walked out the door back towards the barn. As he entered the upper part of the barn he felt nothing but pain and anger. He walked directly to the old table at the far end. He opened the drawer and a bottle of whiskey slid to the forefront.

"Was she right?" he asked of himself as he opened the bottle of alcohol and took a quick swig.

"I am my father." He thought as placed the bottle back to his lips. He turned and walked toward the hayloft. He sat down and drank while commiserating. His sips from the bottle turned into gulps as the alcohol took control of his thinking. Joe was not a drinking man. The painful realizations of his wife's words were too much for him to bear. He could feel the alcohol burning his throat and stomach. He did not stop or attempt to wipe away the whiskey that was dripping down his chin, as his thoughts turned irrational and revengeful.

"This is not my fault," he thought as he tried to kid himself. "I wanted a better life for her, for them." He became overwhelmed with misplaced anger.

He staggered to his feet and meandered to the locked cabinet in the back room of the barn. He opened the door after fumbling for minutes to find the right key. He pushed two shotguns aside and picked out his father's rifle and loaded it. As he placed the bullets in the chamber he thought to himself, "This is all you left me, Pa."

He walked out of the barn filled with rage. He had one thought of vengeance, "Put down the horse, now!"

As he opened the barn door his hands gripped the rifle tighter. The moon shone into the barn from behind him. He approached the front of the young horse's stall, Coffee's stall.

I'll make this right." Joe mumbled to himself. He stepped forward stumbling into the wall. He careened off the wooden sideboard before regaining his balance. He raised the rifle and pointed it towards Coffee; he could see the reflected of the moon through the wide-eyed horse.

Coffee was frozen with panic. Joe did not hesitate. He lifted the rifle and shot twice into the stall. The horse let out an uncommon sound, similar to a child's squeal. The large animal fell to the ground. Joe stood motionless staring into the stall trying to make sense of what he had done.

Tears began to fall down Joe's face as he viewed Coffee, motionless on the floor of his stall. He did not feel sorrow but relief. The overwhelming emotions of the last few hours had caught up with him.

His tears blurred a vision of something bright red in the corner of the stall. He wiped his eyes with his fingers and looked closer at the object.

"It looks like Noah's mitten." He thought of his youngest son for a brief moment.

"What will I tell Noah?" The realization of the pain he will cause the young child struck overwhelmed him.

"I will bury the horse and tell him he ran away. He will not see this, he will never know." Joe weaved another tale of deceit. This one manufactured to protect the vulnerable child.

He walked over to the gloves to pick them up.

"Oh my God!" Joe gasped as he viewed the body of his son.

"It's Noah! What is he doing in this stall?" Joe could not comprehend the events that were rapidly unfolding. He looked over at Coffee's lifeless body then back to the small child who was slumped on the stall floor.

"Noah!" he screamed out to his son.

"Get up! What are you doing in here? You should be in bed!" He yelled at the child who did not respond nor move. Joe fell to the ground and lifted Noah up by his shoulders. He could see a hole in the child's head that had been pierced by one of the bullets. Noah's temple was blown open and flowing with blood, soaking his pajamas. Joe hugged the lifeless body and cried out loud, "No! No! What have I done?"

Blood from Coffee and Noah had now flooded the stall. Joe lay on the floor hugging Noah as the wound continued to flow with blood. Joe's clothes were now soaked in the dark viscous liquid.

"Papa will get you out of here." He said as he struggled to stand with his son in his arms. The blood puddle around his feet caused him to slip and fall, dropping Noah face first into the shallow pond of blood. Joe cried out,

"No!" as he began to panic. He once again scooped up his son and struggled to regain his balance that was altered from the alcohol. The gruesome surroundings caused Joe to lose his sanity.

Joe gave in to the struggle and lay down on the floor of stall sobbing, holding his son and stroking the corpse of Coffee with his other hand.

***

Melinda who was asleep in the house sat up in bed instinctually. She felt nauseous and unsettled. She swore to herself, that she had heard a gunshot or some other form of clamor.

"Maybe I dreamt it?" she said to herself as she looked over at the empty bed beside her. The pillow showed no signs of Joe ever lying on it that night. She stood up and grabbed her robe. As she put it on and tied the belt around her waist she paused,

"There it is again," she strained to her a foreign sound. Melinda could not define the sound but was sure it existed. The only place she thought to inspect was the barn.

"Joe is surely in the barn, doing God knows what." she mumbled to herself.

As she left the house and walked quickly towards the barn the night air was bitter cold. She saw Joe off in the distance. She wrapped her robe up and around her exposed neck and set off on a determined path toward his silhouette. Upon arriving at the spot where Joe stood, Melinda noticed that he was covered with dirt and sweat. She could not understand what he was doing. Joe was shoveling dirt out of a large hole.

"What are you doing Joseph?" She called out to stop him. "Joe!" She yelled his name again. He did not acknowledge her presence.

"This is not right, something is not right." She said to herself. She walked closer to Joe and placed her hand on his shoulder to get his attention as she did she called his name once more.

"Joe! What is going on here?" He stopped and looked at her. Tears streamed down his face leaving a path on his soiled cheek. He did not speak. The look on his face was that of shear insanity. Melinda did not feel in danger, but she felt something was horribly wrong. She moved closer to him to investigate.

"There has been an accident." He said. "Coffee is hurt, I had put him down. I wanted to bury him so the children didn't see." Joe spoke with a detachment that alarmed and disturbed Melinda.

"What are you saying?" screamed Melinda in frustration. "Hurt, how can he get hurt, he has been in the barn all day!" she looked at the hole, then back at Joe.

"Did you call the vet?" she asked him.

"No," Joe responded.

"How did you put him down?" Melinda was becoming even more disturbed by Joe's lack of explanation.

"Is this Coffee's blood?" she asked him with panic in her voice. "Oh my God, Joseph! What have you done?" she stepped backwards away from Joe in shock and horror. She turned and started running desperately towards the barn. It seemed that every pounding step she took jarred her body deeper into the nightmare. She opened the barn door fearful of what she would find.

Once inside, Melinda stood and stared at the blood that formed a glass-like surface over the entire stall. It overflowed into the hallway. The trough that ran down the center of the building flowed with blood. Melinda choked and then vomited from the wretched odor of the blood.

She forced the strength into her body to open the stall and look inside. As she opened the door she hoped that would see Coffee standing in the corner eliminating the possibility of his death.

As her eyes scanned the empty stall she did not see the horse. All that was noticeable was a pile of clothes in the corner. She stepped up and onto the ledge to avoid stepping in the blood. She made her way to the pile of clothes but was having difficulty comprehending why they were there. She was curious as she reached down to pick up Joe's coat.

"Why would he take off his coat and leave it in this stall?" she thought. As she lifted the coat off of the bloody floor she noticed Noah's gloves.

"Why are Noah's gloves in here? God! What is going on?" She said out loud then noticed that it wasn't just Noah's red glove, in actuality it was Noah's arm. She moved quickly, stepping into the pool of blood. She threw the coat off of the figure. Noah was lying under it. His hair was matted and clumped together as if someone had been stroking his forehead. He was in his pajamas. The white flannel imprinted horses on the fabric were stained deep red. She lifted his body unable to utter a sound. She was incapable of registering the reality that her son was dead. As she lifted his body she saw the hole that pierced his small angelic face. His complexion was white and his skin cold. His lips were pale gray and his small fingernails were purple. She pulled his limp body to her chest. She pressed her lips onto his as if to give his motionless body life. She was now soaked with his blood. Melinda did not speak, she did move, she could not loosen the grip she had on her baby. She reacted much the same as Joe did several hours earlier. She lay in the stall holding Noah's body.

The two of them felt a void that would never again be filled. The child she conceived in this very barn had died an untimely, unimaginable death after 9 years of life.

By now, Joe returned to the barn and walked over to Melinda who was still sobbing over Noah's body. He knelt over and gently picked her up. She allowed him. She did not have the wherewithal to fight him or turn her thoughts away from Noah. He pulled her close and cried with her. The two stood in the stall clinging to one another exchanging sorrow.

Melinda pulled away and spoke, "Joseph Bauchmann, I deserve to know what happened, tell me what happened?" she begged him.

The immense pain he felt was etched on his face as he spoke to her.

Joe told Melinda of the events that occurred earlier that night.

"I didn't know he was in here." He looked at her. "I will never forgive myself Melinda. What have I done?" He started to cry out loud. He was willing to suffer all consequences that his selfish and impulsive actions caused.

Melinda felt his pain and sorrow in her heart. Her mind played out several possibilities to explain the event.

"We will have to call the sheriff, Joe. It was an accident." This she knew in her heart. Joe did not try to convince her of his innocence or attempt to rally empathy for his fate. He just shook his head in affirmation.

Melinda thought of her family and their future. "This has to be an accident that we can prove Joe." He listened intently to her speak.

"Noah had to have been kicked by the horse." She stopped and looked at the ground.

"Find the bullet and go get something to strike Noah's head with." Joe looked at Melinda in shock of her request. She was collected and spoke as if she knew exactly what needed to be done.

"Strike his head, with what?" He asked himself.

"If I am to make this look like an accident, where was Noah kicked? The sheriff will surely inspect his head for marks. I already dismembered Coffee." Joe walked out of the barn playing out all possible scenarios. He reached the gravesite where Coffee was dismembered and buried. It was with great determination to bring this horrific incident to a close that Joe jumped into the hole and searched through horse's body parts to find Coffee's hind leg. Once found, Joe climbed out of the grave and went back to the barn. This one act started a ripple effect throughout the farm. Himself, his family, and all future generations felt ramifications.

CHAPTER ONE

The Twitch

The damp air and grey sky set a somber canvas as it always had for Peter at this time of year when the last remaining leaves clinging to the trees fall victim to the harsh winter winds. The trees are left bare, vulnerable and lifeless much like he felt when the winter months come so close after summer starts. It could have been the time of the year, the scenery of the manicured pasture or it could simply be the twitch that Peter had secured underneath the sole of his shoe. Peter made the twitch similar to the ones used by farm hands to secure around a horses nose to keep them still. The theory was simple. The animal, a horse mainly, would concentrate on the pain inflicted from the rope being twisted around their upper lip rather than focus on other external factors. The twitch was brought out normally when the veterinarian was administering a shot. Peter had removed the twine from the wooden handle and replaced it with piano wire.

"Butcher, you understand the problem at hand, right?" Aces spoke to Peter without turning his head to look at him.

Butcher had been Peter's nickname since adolescence. He now answered to the name out of habit. He often thinks back at the first time he heard the name and how it enraged him.

"Fuck you, you wacko. You're like your old man, aren't you? Bauchmann-the-Butcher," Peter can hear the taunts but cannot recall the face of the boy who donned him with infamous nickname. He did not know at the time that the name was destined to follow him for the rest of his tortured life.

"I understand that Shaggy's bein' watched." Peter replied to Aces' question. Peter's thoughts were somewhere else. He did not want to anger his boss, so attempted to refocus his attention.

"He is indeed, and not by just anyone. He has Coatsville's finest spyin' on his ass. The snitch tells me that he paid Shaggy a little visit last weekend and that stupid fuck let him in. He must be breathin' in too much of his own fucking product." As Aces spoke the crevices on his forehead became more pronounced.

"Did you set it up, or did the cops?" Peter asked Aces.

"I did." Aces replied.

"I'd been hearin' stories that the narc cops were watchin' the farm. Fucking Shaggy knows better than to answer to anyone but us." Aces paused, "He's a fuckin' asshole."

Peter did not reply. He shook his head as the two continued to travel the winding back roads that lead to the farm where Shaggy was cooking the methamphetamine.

"Where we meetin' him?" Peter asked Aces.

"The bar down the street, Big T's. T knows we're comin'," Aces replied.

"Look, don't go fuckin' losin' it too much. We need to get him to understand the risk but he still needs to be able to make the product." Aces instructed Peter.

"Fine, if you didn't want action though Aces, you wouldn't be bringin' me. I'll keep it light." Peter replied.

"Are you doin' alright?" Aces asked Peter as he stared out at the road. Peter had known Aces since he was a teenager. Aces was a decade and a half his senior. He looked upon him as a father figure. Aces, was tall and thin with long gray hair that was always pulled back into a greasy ponytail. He shaved rarely.

He smoked cigarette after cigarette leaving the tip of his fingers yellowed and his nails jaundiced and crusted with dirt.

"Yeah, why?" Peter looked over at him as he spoke. The comment was a rare act of sentiment for Aces. Out of all the members in the gang only Peter shared this relationship with him.

"I know this time of year is hard on you." Aces replied showing only a margin of empathy. "Just don't let it fuck your head up. We have jobs comin' up and I need you clear." Aces quickly refocused the sentimental moment back to business.

"I am fine," Peter assuredly responded to Aces to restore any lost confidence he may be feeling about his ability. Peter knew that this was as far as the father-son conversation would go.

The two reached the old single room bar and parked out front. The white aluminum siding was yellowed and dirt covered the building. The windows had been painted over with black spray paint. Aces opened the door and stepped out of the truck. Peter reached down and grabbed the twitch and walked around the truck to the door.

There was one car in the parking lot other than theirs. It was a 1990 rusted blue Honda. The car belonged to Shaggy.

As the two men entered the small, dark, smoky room, the bartender yelled out to them,

"They arrive." He did not ask the two what they were drinking, he poured two shots of Jack Daniels and two draft beers.

"Where is he?" asked Aces.

The bartender tilted his head toward the bathroom.

"He has been in there since he got here. Shit'in himself I'm sure," He laughed as he slid the drink to Aces, then to Peter.

"Butcher, how the hell are you?" The bartender held out his hand. Peter reached out and shook it.

"Doin'," he replied.

At that moment a tall thin man with a sallow complexion walked out of the bathroom. He carried no extra weight and looked at the ground as he walked nervously toward the bar.

"Aces," Shaggy held out his hand in respect to Aces.

Shaggy did not acknowledge Butcher yet.

"Shaggy, we need to talk." Aces spoke firmly.

"Let's go to a table." He placed his hand on Shaggy's shoulder.

Shaggy looked over at Peter but did not look up into his face. "Butcher." He greeted him with the one word.

Aces pulled out a tarnished brass framed chair with ripped red leatherette covering.

"Sit Shaggy." He projected his eyes down toward the chair as he gave the command. Shaggy sat down.

"Seems you've had a visitor at the farmhouse?" Aces questioned him.

"Yeah—" This is all he was able to say before he was quickly silenced from speaking any further.

"He was one of my snitches you stupid fuck. You have one fucking job to do. You are a chemist, a cooker. Not a salesman. Do you understand that?" Aces pointed his finger within inches of the man's face. As Aces spoke, Peter grabbed the man's left hand and slipped the piano cord around his hand. With one swift movement, he circled his wrist and the loop at the end of the club tightened around Shaggy's hand, just at the base of his fingers. He stopped once the string became buried in Shaggy's skin.

Aces continued, "If I wanted you to sell your product, you would be out on the streets, but you're not. We hired you because of your degree. If I hear that you let another fucking person in that door, the building with you in it, will be blown to Fishtown, understand?"

When Aces was finished with his last word, Peter flipped his wrist again. The line sunk even further into Shaggy's hand and a line of blood surfaced.

"I understand, I understand." Shaggy replied as he shifted in his seat bending his skeletal frame toward his bleeding extremity. Peter flipped his wrist once again shortening the loop even more on Shaggy's hand. The band cut into the small finger of the chemist as blood now dripped onto the table.

"Butcher, let up," Aces instructed Peter.

"Yeah, fuckin' let up Butcher," Shaggy repeated Aces directive.

In one swift move, Peter flipped his wrist the opposite direction and the loop loosened and fell off Shaggy's hand. Once the piano string loop was free, Peter tossed the wooden handle of the twitch into the air rotating it one hundred and eighty degrees before catching it. He caught it at the end that was covered in blood and swung the club into Shaggy's ribs, like he was swinging a baseball bat.

"I don't take fuckin' orders from a crankhead. Understand?" Peter spoke through his clenched jaw striking the man's ribs once again.

"Butcher!" Aces called out sternly.

"Back off," he commanded. Shaggy fell to the floor below him in a fetal position. Peter looked at Aces with contempt but followed his directives. He kicked Shaggy once in the ribs before walking away as he mumbled,

"Want a Scoobie snack, Shaggy?"

Aces spoke up, "Shaggy, let this be a learning lesson to you. If I have to come back out here, none of us will be pleased." Aces turned toward Peter. He motioned to him with his eyes to go to the bar and wait for him.

Peter walked to the bar and downed his beer in one long gulp. Aces walked up behind him.

"Let's go outside."

The two walked out the door.

"What the fuck are you doin' Butcher? I thought you said you had your head?" Aces stood within inches as Peter as he spoke his face became red and his blood vessels enlarged.

"We need that fuckin' cunt to use his hands. We need him to finish this order. I doubt he can do that know, with fuckin' cracked ribs." Aces words condemned Peter's actions.

"I don't fuckin' let junkies talk to me like I'm a piece of shit Aces. No disrespect, but he had it comin'." Peter defended his actions once again.

"Fuck him. He'll get over it." Peter looked at Aces without moving his eyes off of his face. Aces was annoyed with Peter's lack of self-control but gave him latitude. Aces relaxed his posture, moved his eyes off Peter's face and onto the truck.

"Take the truck back to the cabin. Cool the fuck off. I'll meet you there later tonight." Aces handed Peter the keys to the truck. He did not shake Peter's hand nor leave him with any closing sentiments. He turned and walked back into the bar.

Peter walked to the driver side door, opened it and threw the twitch on the seat. As he drove back to the cabin, the cold dark air, winding farm roads and the bloody twitch provoked him to think about the tragedy at Brown Hill Farm. He is transported back to the barn where he spent most of his childhood working with his father. Peter's was terrified of his father, Joe Bauchmann. He describes his father as "a pent up man who lived a life sparse in memorable events but full of misfortune." He felt that his father only tolerated him. He lived with the wrath of his father's personal disappointment projected at him.

"Peter," Joe called out. He had a habit of always calling his son twice. The first call was loud and sharp. It was intended to startle him. The second shout was to give the necessary directives.

"Peter, put the bit on that horse and wrap his leg to run." Joe gave Peter his instructions.

"Okay Papa." He responded without hesitation. Once inside the stall he patted the horse on the neck.

"Hello Coffee." He paused for a few moments to stroke the shiny copper-colored horse.

"Today is the day. I hope you do well." He whispered in his ear as it twitched from the warm air of Peter's breath. Peter spent more time than necessary in the horse's stall. He considered Coffee to be his pet and not a farm animal. He grew anxious and fearful that his father would notice that he had spent almost twenty minutes in the horse's stall. That was more time than allotted.

"He's ready Papa, want me to lead him out?" Peter asked his father.

"No. I'll take him. Git out here and sweep this hall." His father responded, coldly.

Peter feared that Coffee would once again be lame. This would mean that the horse would have to be put down. He was filled with stress and anxiety as he watched his father walk the young horse out to the paddock.

He recalls nervously trying to get back to his chores. He wanted to stand and watch Coffee run, but he knew that if he was caught his father would reprimand him. Once Peter swept the entire hall he paused for a moment and glanced out the window that flanked the far end of the barn. He noticed his younger brother Noah, waving to him from his bedroom window. This small gesture placed a smile upon his face. He stopped and pressed his lips against the window blowing out air through his lips spreading them out onto the glass and distorting his cheeks. He loved to make Noah laugh. Warm, happy moments such as this were small gifts to him from Noah.

It was a priceless memory that would forever be burnt into his brain.

Peter realized that he was smiling, as he looked at himself in the rear view mirror. He looked back at the road and recognized the landmarks indicating that the turnoff to the cabin was approaching. He looked back at the clock in amazement that an hour had passed. He reached the small secluded cabin and grabbed his twitch. He climbed the timber stairs as he reached into his pocket for the keys to open the door. He was still preoccupied with the farm although he was back in reality. His childhood memories refused to loosen their grip on him.

As he entered the cabin he flipped the light switch and illuminated the sparsely decorated, damp room. He walked over to the refrigeration, opening it and grabbing a beer from the top shelf. He twisted the cap and threw it into the sink. He pulled the chair away from the kitchen table and sat down to still engrossed with the past.

"Peter."

"Peter, come get your brother off the fence and quit your lollygagging." He heard his father's sharp and short command as clear as the day it was said, twenty-seven years ago.

Peter recalled seeing his father crack the long whip at Coffee, moving him forward. He remembers seeing Noah standing on the bottom rung of the timber rail. His red woolen gloves wrapped around the top rail in a tight grip for balance. A red woolen hat pulled down over his tiny ears.

Noah stood looking onwards peering through the rails at the shiny copper colored horse, quietly in his own universe. Although Noah was always silent and distant the young horse seemed to memorize him. He was never formally diagnosed with an illness. It was evident though that Noah was not the same as everyone else. Noah seemed to be trapped in his own world. He was not deaf and there was no physical ailment. The family and neighbors came to understand Noah as strange and different. Only Peter recognized the relationship that Noah and Coffee shared.

Peter can still hear his father calling out to Noah.

"Noah, stand back off that fence. He could kick up at ya."

Noah did not answer and did not move off the rail. He was preoccupied with the movement, sounds and presence of Coffee. Peter saw how Noah watched the horse's movements.

"Peter, I told you to come git your brother off the fence." Joe called out to him a second time.

His father did not wait for a response. Joe picked up the long whip and snapped it within inches of the young horse's rear end, lunging him forward.

The next memory Peter recounts is the vision of Noah struggling to stay on the fence. As he ran toward him he could see Noah's feet slipping off of the rough uneven rail. Before Peter could reach him, Noah fell through the rungs of the fence and onto the ground where the horse was running. It seemed likes hours before Peter reached his younger brother.

"Peter!" Aces called out into the silent room.

"Peter!" He said his name again but louder.

"What is wrong with you? I thought you said you were alright?" Aces walked toward Peter who was sitting at the table motionless.

Aces approached the table and threw his keys, cigarette and a wrapper of white powder on the table.

"You better get your head out of your ass. We have another job to do. If the past is fuckin' up your head, tell me and I'll have Dempsey do the next job." Aces questioned Peter. Peter did not respond, he got up and walked to the refrigerator to get another beer. He grabbed two and handed one to Aces.

"I'm fine. Just tired," he replied. As he sat down he continued to speak. "Shaggy pissed me off, the worthless cunt." Aces listened then responded.

"Look, I need to know that you all right." Peter did not look at Aces.

"Look at me," Aces said again.

"I have to meet Dempsey in thirty. I don't have time to sit here and babysit you. Just tell me that you're up for this."

"For fucks sake Aces, how many times do I have to say it, I'm fine, fucking wonderful." Peter's abating patience showed.

Aces stood up and drank from the newly opened bottle of beer, downing it in one.

"If you say so, get some sleep. Keep the blow for the ride to New York." Aces didn't wait for a response. The vacuous look on Peter's face foretold of his inner torment. Aces finished the beer, set it on the table and said,

"I'm outta here. See you at the tin can after the job. Don't let me down son." Aces walked away and turned to the door opening it allowing a sharp wind to invade the room.

Peter noticed the chill but did not respond to the sharp wind slapping against the back of his neck. He remained still. After several minutes, Peter got up and walked back over to the refrigerator. This time he stopped and looked at the picture that was held to the front of the refrigerator door. It was a crude rendition of a stick figure horse in tall green grass with a stick figure of a child stood beside it. He remained fixated on the picture as he sat down at the table. He drank the beer but the alcohol could not enter his blood stream quickly enough to sedate the inner demons that were igniting.

CHAPTER TWO

Unspoken Bonds

Peter realized that too much time had lapsed and he had not slept. It was only hours before he had to leave to meet the group for the next assignment. He pushed away from the table and walked to the bed on the opposite side of the one room cabin. The small cot smelled of the damp moldy air that saturated all the fabric in the room. He sat on the bed and kicked off his boots. He laid back and folded his hands behind his head as he stared up at the ceiling. As he closed his eyes the fading light against the background of his tired eyelids formed a red glow. The red shadow looked like Noah's hat that clung to the ragged edges of the splintered timber post. Peter kept his eyes closed recalling the events of that indelible day. He could see Noah's small fragile body within feet of the running horse. When Noah fell into the paddock the young horse became spooked. It reared up on his hind legs and when he came back to the ground he thrust forward with all his weight. Joe jerked the lunge line pulling the scared horse off balance. Peter grabbed his younger brother's coat and pulled him through the rungs of the fence, back to safety.

"Whoa Coffee!" Joe screamed at the horse in an unsuccessful attempt to calm the frantic animal. Coffee lost his footing and too much of his body weight depended upon the weak, healing front leg. The horse skidded, slid, and fell to the muddy ground.

The horse rolled over and leapt back onto its feet within seconds. He stood motionless with his front left leg lifted in the air.

Peter looked at his father who lowered his head to the ground in defeat. Noah was crying. Peter scooped him up into his arms and carried him to the house. Peter saw Coffee from the corner of his eye, failing to place weight on the injured front leg. He felt fear in the pit of his stomach. He knew the fate of the horse. He kept walking toward the house with Noah. He did not want Noah subjected to the misplaced aggression of his father. Noah clutched his brother's neck as the two hastened their pace to the house. Noah was peering over the back of Peter with his head resting on his older brother's neck with his eyes fixed on the limping horse. Peter could feel small drops of water running down his neck. His eyes also filled with tears.

"Have your ma call Vet Fonder, Peter." Joe screamed out him as he reached the door. Peter did not answer his father, he continued to open the door and enter the house with the sobbing child.

Peter woke to the sound of his cell phone ringing. He reached into his pocket and answered the phone.

"Yeah," he mumbled.

"Shit, shave and get out the door you prick." Replied Dempsey. "Aces told me to call your sorry ass and make sure you make the date."

"Fuck you, I'm leaving now." Peter disconnected the call and looked at the microwave, squinting to bring the time into view. The nightmares of his past kept him from obtaining the much-needed sleep that he lacked.

He walked over to the table and dumped the packet of cocaine left by Aces. He snorted two large lines before placing a coffee cup over the remaining pile of powder. He walked out of the cabin, shutting off the lights and locking the door. As he descended the stairs he did not look behind him. He was all too conscious of the fact that he would be spending an extended amount of time holed up in the isolated cabin.

CHAPTER THREE

The Paths We Take

Peter took one more long slow drag from the cigarette that was burnt down to the tips of his fingers. He shook his head in disgust as he flicked the butt to the ground. He had been waiting for hours at the prearranged meeting spot, in a strange place, in an unfamiliar town in an unknown state.

The chilled night air was foretelling of the upcoming winter months.

"Aces was right," Peter thought to himself. "This time of year fucks my head up." He pulled another cigarette out of his pocket and lit it.

"How the fuck did I wind up here?" he said out loud. He reached behind his neck and pulled the tie securing his long hair. He shook his head several times then raked his hands through it, then fastened the tie again around the smoke scented ponytail that hung low on his back.

As he continued to sit in the foreign environment, he vividly recounted the seconds that seemed like years erasing his youth and altering the course of his life. A stumble into a place, at a moment in time, not meant for witness. The ill-fated timing changed everything in his life from that second forward like tumbling dominoes, angry actions led to violent reactions. He still cannot assuage his pain and reason away the awaking from sleep at that specific moment. He cannot answer the question, why he woke up and went into his mother's room instead of rolling over and going back to sleep. Peter recalls entering her bedroom to find it empty. His instincts incited him to go in search of her. He checked every room of the house before going outside to call for her. When opened the door to the outside, the air struck his face seemingly preparing him for the next few minutes, hours, days or maybe even for the rest of his life. Peter could see the glow of a white light in the barn. He made his way devoid of rational thought. Ambiguity did not stop his pace, for an unknown reason he was drawn to the barn. He stopped once he reached the light shining though the barn window. As he held his hand to his face brining the figure into focus, the nebulous outline revealed his father, holding a brownish club, of some sort. He was covered in red soot and muddied clay. His hair was matted and sticking up from his hands grasping at it. His father looked crazed and deranged. The club was raised above his head; he hesitated then fell to his knees. Peter watched intently at his father crying into his dirty, wet hands. He watched without motion or breath. Staggering to his feet, his father rose from his knees to raise the club overhead a second time. This effort was successful, as the club smashed down to the floor. He could not see the floor level from his view. His father was hitting something in a downward motion not in swinging, clubbing motion but in a movement similar to driving a digging bar into the ground. His father was at the edge of Coffee's stall.

"Where is Coffee?" Peter tried to make sense of the vision.

Peter continued to stand outside as a slight rain now drizzled downward from the clouds, casting a fog throughout the valley. His eyes fixated on the club in a frantic effort to decipher the object. Peter suddenly saw the object for what it was. He stepped back away from the window in an instinctual effort to move away from the horrific sight.

"God, it's an animal's leg, there is a hoof." He screamed as loud he could within the confines of his confused mind.

"It's not a club. Look again, it couldn't be a hoof! You have this wrong." He continued in his efforts to decipher the object. He moved back to the window this time keeping a distance between him and the foggy pane of glass. He glared inward again toward the faint light revealing his father's movements.

"It's a leg! It was a horse's leg! Coffee?" Peter leaned in closer. He looked down at the stall floor rising onto his toes to leverage himself into a position where he could view the object that lay on the ground beneath the horse's leg.

The sight that registered in his brain was unthinkable. It was the limp, blood soaked body of his beloved young brother, Noah. Peter was impacted with a feeling of nausea and perspiration was collecting on his forehead and on the back of his neck. His fear rendered him motionless, stood in clear view where he was witness to his father's portentous actions. His body was not in sync with his mind. He was not moving or attempting to flee. He was afraid that his father would see him, afraid to look and too afraid to run.

"Run, go now!" his instincts demanded of him. Without further hesitation Peter turned and volantly ran faster than he had ever ran in his life, back through the cold foggy air to the house. By the time he reached the door to the house he stopped and collapsed, falling to his knees. He grabbed the wet grass as he threw up stomach bile virulently, attempting to cleanse himself of atrocity. Once Peter was inside the house he mindlessly ran up the stairs skipping every other tread. He reached the safety of his room and without hesitation he turned the door knob, entered his room and locked the door behind him. Peter lay in bed in a catatonic state. Panic overtaking his being.

"What did he do? Why did he do it? Why would he be hitting Noah with...?" He could not repeat it. Although he could not say it he lay there in bed unable to remove the indelible sight of his father hitting his younger brother in the head with Coffee's severed leg.

"He's a murderer. Are we safe? Ma? Where was she?" he refused to contemplate the possibility that his father had harmed his mother as well as Noah.

"I have this wrong. This is not happening." Peter convinced himself for the moment, that he did not actually see what his mind is convinced of.

Suddenly he heard voices. He sat up filled with fear. Although panic struck his body, he strained to recognize the muted tones.

"It's Ma." He figured out immediately. He was comforted for the moment. Then overlapping the paregoric sound of his mother's voice was that of his fathers. Peter did not strain to hear their conversation. He felt comforted in the fact that he heard his mother's voice and that he did not denote danger to her or Bonnie and lastly himself.

Peter was not accustomed to violence in any form. The events that had unfolded were aberrant to his childhood and adolescence life in the Bauchmann household. This made it even more difficult for him when piecing together the events that left him confused and vulnerable.

Morning came and Peter was the first of the children to descend the stairs. What should have been a trivial daily task became an event of ambiguity. In the kitchen, his mother, father and Sheriff Stowes were talking. When he entered the kitchen they ceased speaking to one another.

Sheriff Stowes just stood in the corner with his hands in his pocket he did not speak nor look directly at Peter. Melinda was sat at the table and Joe was stood on the other side of the room with his hands down to his side in an unnatural, awkward stance.

"Peter, there was terrible accident last night. Sit down." his mother spoke to him in an unnatural, manufactured tone. "There was an accident last night with Noah. He must have been in Coffee's stall and spooked somehow. Coffee trampled him."

Peter did not know what to say or how to react.

"That's not true." he wanted to shout in response but was too afraid of the ramifications.

Peter looked over at the sheriff who did not offer an objection. He realized that the sheriff had obviously bought his father's version of the events. He turned his head and looked at his father with tacit judgment, pain and anger. His father did not look at him; His eyes were focused on the sugar jar that sat in the middle of the kitchen table.

"Dad is this true? Dad?" Joe did not return a reply.

"Is Noah dead? I want to see him. Where is he?" he was not justified with an answer so he continued with his form of interrogation.

"What did you do to Coffee? I want to see him also. I don't believe you." He spoke now with ardor and conviction to discover the truth.

"Peter, I know this a shock. You can't see Noah, or Coffee. We had to put Coffee down." Melinda spoke to her son with artificial conviction.

"I don't want you to remember him like this or ever see such a sight in your lifetime." Melinda spoke with heart and true passion with this statement. "Please do not tell your sister, I will." She got up from the table and walked toward Peter who stood motionless but tense. She pulled him close and hugged him. This was the first sign of comfort and parental contact he had experienced since the previous day.

"Now go upstairs and let us talk." She said as she stepped back. Peter did not want the feeling of her arms surrounding him in comfort and normality to end.

He obeyed the directive and ascended back up the stairs. The events that followed this indelible moment of his young life were motions entangled in a meaningless drama. His father became immortalized for trying to save his young son and killing the horse out of desperation to save him. He was almost a hero for killing the horse. The overinflated masculinity of the neighborhood farmhands would comment that his actions were justified and honorable. Coffee became the undeserving villain.

From this point forward, when Peter looked at his father, he tried to tell him of his feelings. He looked at him with accusing stares hoping to stir up feelings of guilt. That effort was futile. The rest of his adolescent years were lost from this point forth. He became a misguided teenager with disturbing unexplainable outbursts of aggression. He then became an even angrier disturbed adult. The adoration that he felt for his mother was gone. His instincts always told him that she knew more than she professed to know. He never asked her nor spoke of that night with her. He formed a protective shield over himself as a reaction to his parent's cold detachment abandonment from him and his sister. Peter never questioned either of them. He would never trust them to tell him the truth. He would never again trust anyone with his emotions or feelings. He did not choose to live the life he was living. He told himself that every day. This bitter motivation enabled him to carry out the actions requested of him by the gang he joined. The bikers became his brothers. The leader, his father. The girlfriends his entertainment as no other female figure ever served a purpose of worth. He pledged his love, life and soul to the Skalds after Noah's tragic death.

Peter's unyielding resentment and hostility led him to fame within the gang, as a ruthless and skilled "Enforcer". The "Enforcers" were a group of thirteen men within the Skalds that were sent to perform killings or beatings for retribution. Peter's signature was two clean shots to the back of the head with a double barrel .38 mm. This would guarantee removal of his victims face and prevent identification. He then would knock out the teeth with a hammer and chop off their hands. He would put the hands in a garbage bag and discard the bag at one of two landfills owned by a fellow gang member. If the victim had tattoos, he would fillet the ink image off of their body for guaranteeing the corpse would be identified.

Out of the darkness, somewhere behind him, he heard a voice call out to him.

"Butcher, hey man, good to see you." He turned to see one of his biker brothers, Luko. He was stretching his hand out from his Harley Davidson as he scooted the idle bike toward him.

"Butcher, what the fuck man? Are you here with us or lying on some fucking beach in Florida?" Luko asked him as he slapped his back jarring him from his thoughts. The bitter reality of the upcoming events flooded back into his consciousness.

"The others are already at the bar. We have to go." Luko urged Butcher into action. It was a cardinal rule that the members never used another member's real birth name. Each member had an anointed nickname as to protect their identity. This rule was strictly enforced for the member's anonymity. As the two started their bikes, Dempsey arrived.

"You two bitches know what to do right?" He spoke to the two as if he doubted their talent. "Here, this is for confidence." Dempsey threw a small baggy of coke at Butcher's chest. He caught it before it fell to the ground. Without acknowledging Dempsey, Butcher opened the opened the plastic bag and stuck his finger inside and placed it onto his tongue. Butcher held the baggy up to his nose and inhaled deeply. He was not concerned with the quantity of consumption—as much as he could inhale was adequate.

He handed the remainder of the coke to Luko.

"Thanks Dempsey, not that I need any more fucking balls." He mockingly replied to Dempsey.

"Let's do this." Butcher called out to Luko who was holding his nostrils shut and inhaling.

"See you at the tin can, Aces will be waiting." With this final comment, Dempsey turned his bike around and drove off in the opposite direction.

The line of Harley Davidson's at the bar looked like chrome dominos. Peter's heart was pounding so hard and fast that it resonated in his head. The coke he snorted earlier gave him a rush of adrenalin. This rush pumped through his veins giving him the encouragement needed to carry out his assignment that night.

As he entered the bar, he hesitated for a brief moment; he had a premonition that something would go wrong that night. He brushed off the feeling and thought about the bond he shares with his brothers.

In reality his family was a group of bikers whose life was dedicated to carrying out the ill conceived mission of drug trafficking, extortion and gambling. When Peter's alter ego, Butcher, commanded his presence his actions were vindicated. Peter, however, knew that he could have been more. Every time he stepped back into the shoes of Butcher, he momentarily recounted the night that changed his destiny and thrust him into the life he now led. Neither Peter nor Butcher, although one in the same, had the ability to recognize the relevance of replaying Noah's death every time his alter ego emerged.

Peter knew his role. He was number one in the gang's enforcement team. With the tire iron in his pants, he was prepared to show all the meaningless faces in the bar that night that the person they sought was worthless. Betraying the Skalds meant a fate of pain, humiliation and ultimately death. He had carried out this mission countless times before and tonight was no different.

He entered the bar with three of his "brothers". As they entered, Tiny, who was actually six foot two, spotted the mark and gestured via repositioning his bandana, to Butcher. They all sat at the bar stools adjacent to the mark. That meant moving one patron who already took up residence on the stool. Tiny tapped the stranger on the shoulder and pointed with his thumb gesturing for him to move. Given the size and appearance the stranger quickly accommodated his request.

Butcher sat directly beside the mark and Jackal sat on the other side of him. Butcher called out for the bartender,

"Five Jack's." This meant five shots of Jack Daniels. Iron did not turn to look at the voice for he knew it well. The Bartender returned with five shots filled with the amber colored liquor. Butcher slid one in front of Iron, one to Luko, Tiny and Jackal.

"So, Butcher, this is it? I was wondering when I would see you. I guess tonight is my night." Iron spoke with confidence as he stared straight forward as if looking at Butcher would render him in more danger. Butcher did not answer him. He raised his shot glass up and Luko, Tiny and Jackal all raised their glasses. The men held the shot glass into the air aimed at the bar in front of them, without looking at one another. They all paused, for a fleeting moment offering up a "silent" toast. The members perform this ritual before doing a shot of alcohol. It bears honor to all of their brothers who have pearled. In this case, for the brother who died as result of Iron's turn of faith and breach of oath to the gang. The four men downed the shot and smacked the empty shot glass back onto the bar. The glass in front of Iron remained untouched by him. Tiny called for the bartender to pour three more. Jackal turned to Iron,

"Aren't you drinking with us tonight? You mother fucker."

While Jackal was speaking Butcher calmly and inconspicuously reached forward into his pants and removed the tire iron. He raised the iron with concise speed and muscle. He did not stop to think about the mark, who had been a brother and friend for the last five years. His actions had clear justification, in his mind. Iron, a.k.a. the mark at this unfortunate time, had turned names into the fed's in turn for avoiding prosecution. The FBI was currently showing an interest into the gang's organized business. He gave enough information for the feds to prosecute two members of the gang on racketeering, extortion and attempted murder. The time was now to make a stand and show all those who socialized with Iron that the chains of brotherhood should not but most importantly would not be tolerated.

Butcher struck Iron across his left temple with a single swift blow, blood spattered across all within a five foot radius while splitting his head open revealing his skull and dislodging his left eye from its socket. Butcher laughed out loud at the irony of sticking Iron with an iron.

"The stupid fuck." he thought to himself.

"Fuck you." He said out loud as he kicked him in the face with his hard-soled boot. The other members served as guardians for the rest of the crowd or patrons shielding him from any irrational person who could possibly attempt to interfere with the business of the night. Iron fell to the ground without knowing what hit him. Flashes of Coffee's severed back leg hitting his younger brother's head flashed in his head as he struck Iron over and over again. Peter did not use his .38 mm for this job. He was instructed to send a clear message. Split Iron's head open and spill his brains out in front of the crowd with a tire iron. The message that Butcher sent was crystal clear.

Every scene was comparable in violence although different in method. Butcher was carrying out Peter's re enactment of his father striking Noah. It was some unorthodox predestined play that he forced himself to relive every time his services were being performed. He willing volunteered. He was the best at his job for this one reason.

Iron slumped to the floor while his head continued to drain blood. The crowd scrambled for the exit doors. This scene took seconds to unfold. Butcher and his brothers calmly made their way to the door as he shoved the tire iron back into his pants. Once in the parking lot the men jumped on their Harleys and the sound of engines screaming filled the parking lot as they all drove away in synchronicity.

As Peter drove away from the bar in front position of the other bikers, he did not feel remorse, sorrow or regret. He did, however, feel one step closer to his death. A feeling that completely overwhelms him after each hit that he performs. Peter had a resonating sense that the odds would one day stack against him and he would come to be the mark. He inadvertently was fulfilling this prophecy as a form of self-destruction. His mind drifted to thoughts of Noah. Peter felt as if his life was separated into three chapters. The one he was living, the one when Noah was born and the one when Noah died. Noah's birth caused the family dynamics to change. His condition demanded so much attention for everyone. His father favored him and overcompensated for his autism. Peter felt like the workhorse of the family. Noah continued to demand attention even after his death. The family did not share evening dinners, his father never ate at the dinner table with the family from that point on.

His mother and father did not speak as if they were husband and wife. Peter spent the majority of his life wondering what the purpose of it all was.

His conclusions always arrived at the same place.

"This is my destiny." He would say to himself in justification. "My life is a waste as I drift in and out of bad connections with fucked up pathetic people." He said to himself as he stared out into the vast dark highway. He felt the constant struggle that seemed to push him into balancing danger, life and death. Peter was a product of his environment. His environment changed his perspectives. Bonnie, his sister did not have the same reaction to the family's misfortunes. She however, was fortunate enough to escape the imaginable sight of Noah being bludgeoning by her father. Although she withdrew in social settings, she went on to become a schoolteacher. She married and had two children. One of which she named Joseph Noah. She never really understood why the accident caused such bitter resentment between her mother and father. Bonnie remained unaware to this day that Peter new the truth of that night. Of all the unfortunate players in this drama of that night, it was Peter that was affected the most. Melinda and Joe were both guilty of abandoning Peter's anguish. Peter never gave consideration to the fact that his father did not know he witnessed the bludgeoning and that his mother was never aware that he ever left his bedroom that night. He refused to let those vital facts alter or abate his anger and feelings of abandonment.

The years that followed were wrought with sadness, disappointments, dreams lost and moments never recaptured. His mother died first, at an early age and his father died four months after she passed away.

His mind was far from the murder of Iron. As usual he gave no consideration to the life that he had just ended. Neither

Butcher nor Peter ever thought of the subsequent consequences of his actions to the victim's family, wife or children. None of it mattered to him. He was cold, vicious and calculated.

The men drove in the dark for two hours until they reached the meeting spot where the president, Aces and Dempsey, the number two man, were already waiting. They were standing around a tin barrel that was ready to incinerate their blood soaked clothing. The two were standing side by side. Dempsey lifted a bottle of Jack Daniels to his lips and drank from it, handing it to Aces who repeated the action. They did not acknowledge the arrival of the others but waited for them to approach them. This was a standard act of dominance amongst Aces and Dempsey. They never went to the lower men; the lower men were obligated to go to them. This was much like dogs in a pack following the natural order of alpha and beta command.

Peter dismounted his bike; his legs were cold and stiff. He stretched and noticed the blood spatter covering his shirt and jeans. What he failed to notice is the blood that had splattered onto his face. He walked to the back of his bike and opened the leather pouch and took out a pair of jeans, t-shirt and leather jacket. He undressed in the cold dark night while his brothers celebrated their victory. He walked over the fire carrying the blood stained clothes.

"Hey mother fucker. What took you so long? Did you stop off for some pussy to celebrate the kill?" Dempsey spoke with sharp sarcastic wit. The others laughed as he walked over to the group.

"The only pussy I want to see tonight is that little fucking whore with the big tits that is decaled on your fucking forearm." replied Butcher as he held out his arms to hug Dempsey in the ingratiating customary greeting. After the cold display of emotion, he turned and stuffed clothes into the rusted metal can and watched as he prodded the clothes downward with a stick handed to him by Luko, who had already disposed of his bloodied garb.

"I am glad to fuck that this is over, may that little mother fucker suck his mother's tits in hell." Peter said as he pulled the metal tab off the beer can that was handed to him by Luko. They all raised their cans and toasted the dead.

"Who got the girl?" asked Dempsey.

"Luko did." said Tiny.

"Luko looked up and said, "What fucking girl?" There was a pause and look of confusion on Luko's face.

"When this kicked off there was no bitch." Luko quickly added sensing Dempsey's demeanor was changing with every word.

"The fucking girl with the mark, you prick." Dempsey snapped back at Luko in anger.

"There was no fucking girl Dempsey." Luko replied in defense.

"Honest Dempsey, the bitch wasn't there, I didn't see her either." Tiny spoke up in an attempt to defend Luko without inciting Dempsey into violence and retribution.

"I was with Luko and Tiny the whole time." Jackal had to speak up at this point and defend their claim.

"Let's quit the bitch slapping ladies, we are goin' nowhere with this." Aces spoke up as the leader with efficacy to smolder the tempers that were flaring. He turned to Butcher.

"Was the bastard's old lady done?" he asked of him.

"I did the mark. She was not my mark. I honestly don't know Aces." Butcher spoke with confidence and arrogance.

"Butcher you fucking asshole." Dempsey interrupted and stepped toward Butcher aggressively.

"You fuck'd up. Let me see the bullets you should be sweat'n over this cock up. If she got away you're proper fucked Butcher." Dempsey continued his emasculation of Butcher.

Aces called out, "Knock it off, both of you." He sounded like a father scolding his bickering sons.

"Are we sure this cunt was there in the first place?" He turned speaking to Dempsey.

"Yes, she was fucking there, probably sucking his dick at the bar and these fucks failed to see her." Dempsey showed zero patience.

"Mark my fucking words this is gonna get someone sent down. And your boy there (he pointed at Butcher) is the cause." Dempsey turned his back toward Butcher and faced Aces.

"And I can fucking guarantee it won't be me." With this final word he threw his beer into the fire and walked away into the darkness. His figure disappeared as his boots sounded his departure against the gravel surface of the dead end road.

The group fell silent. All men stared at the fire either too afraid to speak or make eye contact with the man rubbing his weather-aged forehead. Aces motioned for Butcher to follow him away from the others. He did so without speaking.

Once away from the others, Aces spoke to Butcher in a low tired voice.

"Dempsey was in charge of this hit Peter. If it went wrong it is his reputation that will suffer." He spoke to him as a father trying to smooth bad blood between his two sons.

All the members fully cognizant that Dempsey was working toward the goal of becoming the next Chapter President. All the men involved in this hit were aware that if the girl got away, this would not be favorable on his resume.

"Think, was she there?" Aces questioned Peter.

"No, not around the bar. If she was, she got away before we got up to the bar." Peter responded in an attempt to restore Aces confidence in his ability to do the job, properly.

"You better go back and question your boys on this. Get it through their fucking skulls that she better not had gotten away." Aces spoke then paused and looked over at Peter.

"I will not tolerate a fuck up here. Is that clear?" Aces did not wait for Peter's response.

"Go sort this out while I go talk to Dempsey."

Aces walked away into the same dark space as Dempsey. Aces was more patient and tolerant than Dempsey. It was no secret that the members dreaded the day that Aces stepped down and passed the torch to Dempsey. All knew the group would have a different temperament. Aces was a peacekeeper and Dempsey was an igniter.

Peter walked back to the three that stood in the same spot staring at the blazing barrel.

"You three better hope this cunt didn't get away. If she did I will personally snap each and every one of your fucking arms off and shove them up your asses." Peter spoke with the quiet assured confidence of Aces.

"You two get the fuck out of here and wait until I call you." he pointed at Jackal and Tiny.

"Luko you stay here until it burns down, dump the ashes and roll the barrel into the river." Peter crumbled the can and threw it into the fire.

He walked away from the group that was disbursing. Only Luko was left behind. As he reached his bike Dempsey appeared out of the dark on his own.

"You better hope this does not go tits up you cunt." Dempsey spoke with disdain toward Peter.

"Get the fuck out of here and go to the spot for the next few days. Don't fucking call anyone. I don't fucking care if you're having a heart attack. No one." Dempsey looked directly into Peter's eyes.

"Actually, give me your fucking cell phone." Peter did as he was told without showing any signs of submission. Dempsey placed it on the ground and smashed it with the heel of his boot.

"Pick the SIM card out of that and toss it in the barrel and get the fuck out of here." Dempsey pointed down at the crushed cell phone parts. Without another word he mounted his bike and started it. Dempsey had altered his exhaust to make it exorbitantly loud. It impacted whoever stood nearby. To Dempsey it was his siren that he meant business. The others merely thought him to be a prick. Dempsey was feared, but not respected.

Peter knelt down and sorted through the fragmented plastic until he found the SIM card. He picked it up and walked back to the burning barrel. He walked over and threw the small plastic chip into the fire and waited until he saw it curl and melt in the flames.

He did not look at Luko although he knew he was aware that he had fucked up. He told himself as he walked away, "I just hope the bitch will be too afraid to speak."

Their reprimanding seemed to never end. The realization of the unintentional error weighed heavy on all involved with the hit that night. Peter wanted to stay with his brothers. He was avoiding the trip to the cabin and the long lonely days and nights that stood before him. He walked back to his bike alone and in silence. He mounted his bike and reluctantly started it and set forth on the long drive to the designated safe house. The drive punished him further by affording him isolation and time to recollect on the events of his life. The first three chapters of his life would consume his thoughts in the upcoming days with the first of the three chapters being his time at Brown Hill Farm. He could not escape the events unfolding in the third chapter. This part of his life was still in progress, his life as a Skald.

CHAPTER FOUR

Actions and Reactions

Peter arrived at the cabin after driving for hours in the cold night air. He did not wear a helmet when he rode and the extremities on face felt the effect. The air foretold of imminent snow. Peter opened the door as he called out to the empty room, "Ah, home sweet home."

Peter had grown to despise the amount of time he spent at the cabin, in hiding, after an assignment. He went through his normal routine by pulling out the kitchen chair, then walking over to the refrigerator, grabbing a beer, and twisting off the cap. He turned and tossed the cap into the sink, waiting to see if made it. He allowed the caps to collect, benching marking the time he spent there. The one prerequisite Peter made was to have the cabin stocked with beer, cigarettes and cocaine. The only food he consumed while being held up in there was cans of beef stew and chili. Normally, he did not feel like eating, to him it was not a conventional, spending time there. He drank seven beers before kicking off his boots and lying down on the small bed that smelt of the damp moldy cabin.

Peter dreamt that night of Karen. At the age of nineteen, he felt love for a person, Karen, instead of the empty sociopath emotions that were now his persona. When he was with Karen, he had a life outside of the Skalds. Back then, he was only a courier, transporting methamphetamine, marijuana and cocaine for Aces. He did drug running during the day and by night, he lived a more stereotypical role. Karen's profession was that of a secretary. She tolerated his life, as dark as it was, she turned a blind eye. The two of them had self-serving motives for continuing with the relationship. Peter wanted a grounded life with a loving woman. Karen grew up being attracted to men like her father, unconventional. Karen had a child to another man. Peter tried to play the role of a loving father and devoted fiancée.

This was time when Peter was reluctant to become more entrenched in the gang. He did not want Karen to become communal property. Wives, girlfriends and sometimes sisters, of gang members were commonly shared amongst the members for sexual entertainment. He truly loved and respected Karen and did not to share her with the other men in the gang who had disdain and disrespect for women, that was the common female sentiment.

In Peter's dream he took on the appearance of Aces. He was delivering a package and his cell phone rang. He silenced the ringer, ignoring the caller ID and walked into an abandon house. When he stepped into the house, he was standing in the bar where he clubbed Iron to death.

Details of the dream were incorrect but the storyline was exactly as it was lived out in real life. He was reliving deeply repressed moments from his past.

Once inside, as he was exchanging the product for money, Peter's cell phone rang again. Having a cell phone ring during a drop showed lack of professionalism and experience. Peter had long since learned the proper etiquette, but on this particular drop, he was still ignorant to the protocol. He apologized and turned the phone off.

After the drop was made, Peter sat with the recipients for an hour so, drinking and sampling the product. When he had his fill of drugs and booze, he left the house, turning on his phone as he left the house. There he noticed a message was waiting. He almost did not play the voicemail as he fumbled with small buttons, trying to contain his composure. He listened to the stranger who had left the message.

"Mr. Bauchmann, we have a Karen Smithton here at the emergency room. Please come to Mercy Hospital ER, as soon as possible. There has been accident."

Peter heard the call but disbelieved the message. He replayed it again.

"What the fuck?" he questioned the call, his decision to silence the phone and the probability of the accident.

Peter felt numb as he disconnected the call. He stood beside his bike in disbelief as heart raced from the combination of the drugs and emotional adrenalin caused by the news.

"What will I do if something happens to her?" he asked himself as he navigated through sharp bends that seemed to have no end and red lights that prevented him from speeding to her aide. He avoided running through the red lights for fear that he would be pulled over by the police and fail a sobriety check.

Once arriving at the hospital, he pulled his bike in front, dismounted, and ran inside. He approached the nearest nurse and announced who he was, "I am Peter Bauchmann, I received a call, and Karen Smithton is here. Can I see her?"

The nurse escorted him back to the bed surrounded by a white curtain. Peter flinched as he pulled the curtain aside, fearing Karen's condition. A doctor stood by her bedside, writing on a clipboard, he looked up as Peter entered the patrician.

"Are you her fiancée'? She has been asking for you."

In the dream that Peter was having this night, the doctor appeared in Dempsey's body, sneering at him with a look of approbation as he spoke.

"Yes, I am," Peter responded, "How is she?"

The doctor responded, "She was in a car accident, she is stable, but I am afraid to tell you that I have bad news." Peter looked at Karen who lay motionless and unconscious, hooked up to several monitors.

"The trauma she suffered was severe, causing her to lose the baby." The doctor then turned around and picked something up off of a chair that was off in the corner of the room. As the doctor turned around he was holding the body of a fetus in his hands. The infant was still, with a bloody umbilical cord still attached. The doctor stretched out his arms handing the fetus to Peter, "Here is your dead son," he replied.

Peter reached out and took the infant into his hands, cradling it, rocking it back and forth as he cried, "Please forgive me, my son."

Peter suddenly awoke at this point in his nightmare and opened his eyes. He was dripping in sweat and the sheet on the bed was damp. He sat up, and tried to refocus his mind, unsuccessfully, his mind began recalling the actual events of that night.

That reality was not far off from the version he had just dreamt. He did not analyze the meaning behind Dempsey playing the role of the doctor, or his appearance being Aces. He felt the deep abyss of his sadness as he relived the feelings of the night. He reached over to the end table and picked up his cigarettes, lighting one.

"First Noah, then my unborn child. I am sick to death of loss," he said as he got out of bed to grab a beer. He feared that if he went back to bed at this time, he would continue with the nightmare. This event was a final blow for Peter, another death in his life that sucked all the life out of him. First, Noah, then his son, he decided that night that he would not build another relationship with a woman. He thought back on the night, how it played out in reality.

Once the doctor told him that his son was dead, he sat in the chair, with his head in his hands, and cried. Karen awoke while he was crying and condemned him for abandoning her that night.

"Where were you when they called you? I have been her for seven hours," she said with tears in her eyes. Her pale skin tone dramatized the bruising and stitches surrounded her right eye. Peter stood up and walked over to her. He leaned over and brushed her hair off of her forehead, exposing the stitches. He cried openly and he kissed her forehead.

"I am sorry Karen. I had to take of business, as soon as I received the call, I came." He spoke apologetically to her.

She turned her head away from his direction and stared at the curtain that surrounded the bed. Peter knew at that moment that Karen would not forgive him, he also knew that he would not forgive himself. The accident was not his fault, but it was clear that she needed him and he was not there for her, or his child. He leaned over once more and kissed her on the top of her head and walked out of the room. He walked straight down the hall and out of the front door. He tried to run away from the pain. He could not face Karen again. As the hospital doors slide open he ran out into the night to his bike. He jumped on it, gunning the engine, spinning the tires on the asphalt as he sped away. Peter fled the scene as irrationally and quickly as he could but he could not escape the empty feeling of guilt, loss and sorrow. The life of his son was taken before he could lay his eyes upon him. He would never know him, or what kind of a father he would become. He imaged his son looking like Noah, with dark hair and dark eyes.

He felt frustrated and overwrought with the constant barrage of painful memories.

"What the fuck man," he said to himself as go up and walked across the small cabin to the refrigerator. "I need to get a fucking grip."

Peter knew that the next few weeks were going to be even more difficult if he could not refrain from thinking of his past demons. As he opened the beer and sat at the table he began to think more defensively.

"What happened for a reason. What kind of father would I have been? What kind of husband?" He said to himself as he drank the beer. The Skalds were his sole commitment and dedication from that point forth. He never engaged in another personal relationship. He became more aggressive and recalcitrant towards life.

Peter thought that the accident as an act of fate, that ended what would have been a more conventional life for him. He often thought to himself, "What would have happened to my life if Karen wasn't in an accident that night? What if I was with her instead of makin' a deal?"

Peter's thoughts then turn to Noah and his father, "What would have happened to my life if Noah didn't die? I should've protected him, he needed me, just like all of the others that I let down."

Peter began to spiral deeper into regret and blame. The roads and paths that Peter took always lead back to Brown Hill Farm. He did not want to go back to sleep, he walked over to the coffee pot that sat on the stove. He opened the lid and reached inside, pulling out a baggy of cocaine. Coffee was not a preferred beverage of his, nor that of any visitor he would have. Peter was determined to stay away, for at least awhile. It was only hours after he hit his mark, and hopefully killed him. He thought to himself, "The hit was easier than the nightmares I just had."

He cut two lines on the table and snorted both with the metal straw that he kept in his pocket. As the drugs took affect, he relaxed. He stood up and walked to the window. He observed the snow falling. Softly and quietly the small flakes fell from the dark sky, melting as soon as they struck the ground. He scratched his beard, and stood watching the snow, swirling and falling to the surrounding woods.

He took another beer and walked back to his bed. He lay down, crossing his legs and folding his arms behind his head; he was determined to have a moment of mental respite. He could not change the past and he did not want to change the present. He wanted to escape the mental torment that he suffered, and the drugs combined with the alcohol took care of that.

CHAPTER FIVE

Parallel Happenings

The sun was reflecting off the chrome bumper of the car in front of Rudi, reflecting light into her eyes. Rudi pulled down the visor to shield the glare. She flipped up the mirror and looked at her lipstick to see how much of it had rubbed off onto her coffee cup. She flipped it shut, focused back on the road and realized her mind wondered off the traffic. She stomped on her brakes to avoid from careening into the car into front of her.

"Jackass," yelled Rudi. The highway was crowded and gridlocked as it was every morning at this hour. Rudi despised the daily commute to work. The cars inched along like marching ants, single file, two by two. Rudi glanced over at the car beside her in the HOV lane and noticed the man driving a faded red pickup truck, had a blow up doll sitting in the passenger seat.

"I hope he gets a ticket, asshole," she thought before commenting out loud, "I have to get out this town."

The only consolation sitting in traffic served was that it provided her timeout of a busy day to plan her move, back up North. Luke, her husband called her a dreamer, but Rudi knew in her heart, a move would happen this year.

Rudi was thirty and considered successful by her generation. She was confident and strikingly pretty with black hair and pale blue eyes. She and Luke had lived in Florida for the last seven years. They both found it hard to adapt after he was transferred for his job. At the time, Rudi happily accepted the move as an exciting start to their lives together, but the strangeness to the foreign area wore both of the down.

The two of them were very much in love. They lived in a gated community where the median age was twice that of theirs. They both felt out of place in Florida as native "Northerners". Both missed the change of seasons and celebrating cold weather holidays.

Luke grew up in rural Pennsylvania and Rudi in rural Ohio. They had lived in Florida since meeting in college. Luke was offered a job that would start the two on a path of good fortune and happiness, so they had convinced themselves. At the time, happiness and good fortune had a definitive price tag and they were willing to pay the price of leaving their family, homesteads and regions that provided a comfort zone to both of them. Luke was making good money now and could transfer within the company back north where the pharmaceutical company had offices. Rudi had made up her mind so the daily commute, life and living in the area became more frustration and depressing daily.

"Look at these mindless, wandering souls, destined to live out a life missed." Rudi thought to herself. "They will never acknowledge what is meant for them, where they are meant to be or meant to do." She thought as she stared ahead at the bumper of the car sat in traffic in front of her. "I am meant for more, I will do more, Luke and I will move and make a difference."

Rudi was self consumed and engrossed in thoughts that gave her motivation and comfort. She was aware of the tacit path that her life was meant to take. While she thought of her uncertain future and how it would envelope, she reminded herself that small seeming less meaningless events were constantly unfolding, every minute of every passing day that would inevitably move her toward a place that she knew she was destined to find. Rudi drove slowing in the gridlocked path of strangers, feeling a yearning in the pit of her stomach, so strong it made her impatient and nervous, this was her daily commute.

***

The shiny blue utility vehicle came to a stop in the middle of the road as Lois, looked down at her notes and scanned the mailboxes. She leaned over straining her eyes as she attempted to find the correct address of the house she was sent to inspect for her new sale. She looked to the right and then to the left before deciding to pull into the nearest driveway.

Lois was a typical middle-aged realtor. She grew up in the area and used the local gossip to her advantage to sale homes. She rifled through her files before finding the paper with the Bauchmann information on it.

She pulled a pair of plastic red reading glassed out of the cup holder and slipped then onto her nose.

"Bonnie Bauchmann," she said to herself. "What a sad story to this old farm." She added.

Bonnie Bauchmann contacted Lois to sell the farm. The neighborhood was aware that the house was left derelict in an estate settlement, once Joe Bauchmann passed away.

"This has to be the farm," she said as she struggled to see the old red brick structure through the overgrown landscape.

"It is hardly recognizable," she thought, "This must be it." She said as she placed her file on the seat and put the car back in drive, moving slowing down the long driveway.

As she navigated down the dusty, sparsely stoned driveway the house suddenly appeared, no longer catafalque by the overgrown landscape. The large brick house was weathered as if the years tried to destroy its strength and test its resilience. Lois pulled off to the side and put the car in park. She looked out the window and the house and paused remembering the house as it stood when she was a child. It was the most beautiful house in the town. She recalled playing there with Bonnie when she was a child. Rose bushes surrounded the house, and in the summer, when in bloom, their sweetness filled the air. The front of the house was flanked with 30-foot wooden columns that were always pristine white. Only one stood intact, as the other three were splintered and missing. The front porch had long succumbed to the harsh winter weather.

Lois opened the door and stepped out onto the driveway shaking her head in disbelief. She had as personal attachment to the home as most of the neighbors in town, each with their own interpretation of the tragedy that took place decades ago. It was her personal opinion that Joe Bauchmann lost his mind and intentionally shot the young son, who was mentally retarded, or something like that.

"How am I going to sell this property?" She thought as she redirected her attention to the presence. She looked around the yard without venturing off of the sidewalk.

An abandoned rusty car lay abandon just beyond the house, shotgun holes covered the driver side door.

"How am I going to sell this property? It's overrun with weeds, the frontal view is horrendous and this is the outside," she said to herself as she shook her head. "This is just plain disgraceful." She shook her head in disappointment as she continued to look around at the skeleton home.

Lois navigated her way to the side porch, there was no porch or porch floor leading to the front door of the house. She had been directed by the former owner that the keys would be placed in an envelope and set in between the screen door and side porch door. Lois stepped onto the porch in between the countless black plastic garbage bags that overflowed with aluminum cans. A tin beer can crunched under the heel of her boot as she stepped, startling her, she jumped back and regained her composure.

"Can this get any worse?" She thought, "This is a realtor's nightmare."

As she reached toward the ripped, tattered screen door, a stray cat lunged out from behind one of the stacked garbage bags.

"Oh my," she gasped, as she lost her balance once again. As she grabbing for the banister that framed in the porch she a splinter impaled her finger. She quickly retracted her hand and placed her injured finger in her mouth. The small, thin cat was now rubbing up against the leg of her black nylon pants. The chaos was taking its toll on her patience. She nudged at the cat with the heel of her black high-heeled shoe.

"Shoo." She hissed at it to move away from her.

She bent over and placed her briefcase on the porch floor and reached once again for the door. As the door opened it fell away from the frame and rested on the porch floor. On the step she spotted the envelope.

"Finally, the keys!" she said, rejoicing.

She picked up the envelope to find a single key wrapped in a piece of paper. She unfolded the note to read the content.

"Lois, this is the key to the side door. The attorney handling the estate for my brother and me is James Harrold. His number is 412-555-9990. Please call him with any questions."

Signed, Bonnie Bauchmann

Lois read the note and found the tone strange. Why the rush now to sale this house. It has obviously been abandoned for quite some time. Why would the house be dangerous? I think the porch is a nightmare," thought Lois. With her experience with estate sales and liquidations she assumed that the parent or remaining parent died and now the children wanted rid of the burden. The burden of this farm was long over; no one had maintained it for 10 or so years she said to herself. "God help the people who take on this project. I sure wouldn't want this nightmare." She thought to herself. "But, there is a buyer for everything." She said out loud.

As Lois opened the door she viewed the kitchen. There was no furniture but an old oak family style kitchen table. It looked as if it had always been in the kitchen. The cabinets were opened, if hinged at all, the cupboards were barren. She navigated her way through the entire house noticing the ceiling in certain areas was collapsing. The bedrooms upstairs had old sinks, toilets and bathtubs in them. An old mattress was left in the smallest of the three rooms. A tattered old stuffed horse lay in the center. "That is strange; she kicked the stuffed animal with the front of her shoe". I wonder why this was left. There are no other signs of anyone living here."

She made notes, carefully made her way down the narrow steps where the banister had been removed and made her way for the door. "I cannot show this house until it is made safe for viewing," she wrote on her notepad. She itemized all the hazards one by one.

As she made her way to the porch door her cell phone rang. She stopped to view the number. It was her sister calling. She opened the door while answering the phone.

"Hello Elaine. I am at the end of the viewing the old Bauchmann Farm! Strange you called at this time. Do you remember that beautiful house on the hill in Everstown?

The daughter called me to list it. I am just leaving; I will call you back once I get into the car. Good, talk to you in a just a short moment."

Lois hung up the cell phone and pulled the key from her yellow nylon blazer. She stopped for a moment and tried to brush the white cat hair that had clung to her static filled pants. Unsuccessfully, she locked the door, pushed the screen door shut and walked back to her car. Once inside she started the engine paused for a moment and made a final note,

"I will have Ben Heller from the office appraise the barn." She wrote. "If the house looked like that, I do not want to enter that barn." She commented to herself. She pulled an embroidered handkerchief with her initials on the corner and placed in her mouth to moisten it. She rubbed the mud off the heel of her shoes, picked one or two cat hairs off her black pants then reached for her cell phone to return her sisters call and tell her all about the abandoned ruined Bauchmann Farm and gossip about all the tragedy that this farm had seen. "I cannot image who will buy this place. It will have to be an out-of-towner. No local will take this on, especially with the history of the old place." She concluded before moving on with day.

As Rudi drove home she thought of her childhood home. The day was long and she needed the escape. She remembers as child yearning for that horse. She laughed as she recalled the memory of her and Diane Canton rivaling daily while arguing whose horse was better than whose. Admitting to only herself that it was Carol. She smiled as the sun shone into the window and the heat of the day wrinkled her once neatly pressed shirt. Before she realized it she was pulling into her development. It was early this afternoon. She arrived home at 4:00 P.M.

As she opened the door the humid air caused immediate perspiration to collect on her nose and brow. Rudi said to herself as she mopped her nose with a napkin left in side compartment of the door, "It is already to so damn hot here, I feel like I am in hell." She held out her key and locked the car door. Once home she went into her office and began to move forward and acknowledge the pull that she felt within her. As she reached the door to find a note was stuck to it. The note was from Luke.

"Did you have a wonderful day my princess? I love you. I stepped out for a second but left a pitcher of margaritas on the table. Relax. Be home in minutes."

"I love you, Luke"

She folded up the note and placed it in her purse. She smiled and acknowledged the thoughtful effort made by her husband. She felt the uplifting confidence and security of her marriage. She placed the key in the door and was comforted in the knowledge of being home.

"Home, for now." She said aloud as she went into the bedroom to change.

Rudi changed and spent the next hour or so drinking the margarita's and doing internet searches on the farms, horse sales and articles on caring for horses.

She was interrupted by the vision of Luke entering the back patio caring a bag. She shut the laptop and got up to greet him. She went into the kitchen to pour herself another drink and one for Luke. She set up a tray with the drinks, chips and salsa and slid the patio door open to the pool. As the door slid open, Luke was on the other side.

"Minutes is hours with you." She said to him as she smiled then puckered her lips as she bent forward to kiss him.

"I wanted to buy some things for dinner. Beside I knew you occupy yourself with the Margaritas. And…let me guess, planning our lives. Hey, one hour is enough time for you to plan the rest of our lives." Luke's sarcasm was nothing new.

"Very funny Luke," replied Rudi.

He kissed her on the lips and said, "Let me put this away, change and I'll be right out."

Rudi walked over to the table and set the tray down. She settled down on the chaise lounge and drew a long sip from her drink. She relaxed into the chair and absorbed the warm sun. She closed her eyes and tried to clear her mind of all the recent events. Rudi was cognizant of the constant movement of her internal engines. Downtime was very important to her. She waited for Luke. She closed her eyes for a moment and opened them suddenly to what she thought was the sound of horse. She did not have time to register the odds of the interpretation before she saw a large chestnut horse run into their yard. Thankfully it was stopped by the large stucco wall that encased the entire development. The horse had a saddle but no rider. The reins dangled dangerously low to the knees of the horse. Rudi sprang to her feet and ran to the screen door. "Luke! Luke!" The development where Rudi and Luke lived was in a small town that neighbored a rodeo. Horse walking paths were placed in various parks and along roads. The town was equine-friendly. Rudi wanted to live in the neighborhood for this reason. She often saw people riding horses but never had she seen anything like this.

When Rudi reached for the horse, he was sweated, scared and very anxious. The Florida heat was brazen that day. She slowly walked toward the horse. He was breathing heavily and moving side to side as if he was working out the best path to take to run again. Rudi kept her hands down and spoke softly. "Sshhhhhhh, easy boy." She edged closer. The horse turned toward Rudi and looked at her. His large brown eye filled with fear. "Easy, I won't hurt you, where is your rider?" Rudi spoke softly and soothingly. The horse looked at her but did not try to escape. She was now close enough to grab the reins that were hanging in front of the horses' neck. Once she did the horse jerked his head slightly but not hard enough to pull the reins from her loose grip.

She heard a young boy's voice. "Star Buck!" he yelled. Rudi pulled at the reins to insight the horse to walk with her. He did willingly. He ceased breathing frantically and appeared relaxed. Rudi called out to young boy, "He is over here!" She caught the boy's attention and he ran to them.

"Thank you," the boy said. "I was riding over on 186 and something startled him right as we were passing your development. He reared up and I fell off." The young boy said with a shaken voice. "I was really scared that he would get hit or that I would not be able to find him. This is a big development."

"Can I get you a glass of water? Something for your horse?" Rudi had no clue what to give the horse. If truth be told, Rudi knew very little about horses, care of them or maintenance of them. Luke approached the two of them at this point. "Luke, please get a glass of water for…what is your name?" asked Rudi. Jared replied the small-framed boy. "Luke, please get Jared a glass of water."

"No that is okay, I just want to get back to the stable."

"Are you okay to ride him again? Rudi was concerned.

"I will just walk him. I am okay."

Rudi was not comfortable allowing the boy to leave walking the horse by himself after the events that had just unfolded. "Can you call someone at the stable to help you? Your parent's maybe?"

"No, I am okay". The boy seemed embarrassed and just wanted the ordeal to end. Rudi could not convince the boy that he needed assistance.

He tugged at the reins and the horse willingly walked with him with his head low.

"Thanks for your help," and the boy walked away as if he faded into the summer haze.

"What, you are the horse whisperer now that you want to buy an old horse farm?" Luke laughed and prodded Rudi's ribs. "That was really, really freaky, can you believe that? What are the odds? This is a sign!" Rudi was out of breath from speaking so fast and the excitement of the incident. As the two of them walked back to their backyard, she continued to prate on about the scenario. "Yeah, a sign to stay away from horses. They are crazy in the head," Replied Luke. Rudi did not respond to the comment, she did not even hear him at this point. She was engrossed in the moment and consumed with the belief that this was a sign.

"Luke, like an hour ago I was researching horses and how to handle them. I have been so nervous that I cannot handle them. I have never had a horse. I can do this, I can handle them."

"Rudi, there is no doubt in my mind that you can handle them. I just think they're dangerous."

"Yeah, they can be. But so can those speed bikes that you love so much!" snapped Rudi in defense.

"Touché'," Luke reached out and opened the screen door for Rudi. "I need another drink," Luke said with a tone of exasperation.

CHAPTER SIX

Destined Introduction

Rudi leaned over her side of the bed and bit Luke on the neck. He sprang around and jumped on top of her, they both laughed like children. "Good Morning", she replied. "What is on your Saturday agenda Master Luke?"

Rudi had been awake for the last 40 minutes obsessing over the plans to buy a farm in the North East and move from South Florida. She was going to bring it up to Luke once he was focused and awake. She thought of buying a horse farm and buying some horses. She had no idea how to go about it but common to Rudi she jumped in with two feet and figured details out later. She had a gift for winging her way through situations once she put her heart to it. Rudi did not have any experience with horses. Since the age of five she had tried to convince her mother and father to buy her a horse. Without the means and property that wish was never granted. Rudi grew up longing to own a horse. She laughed to herself as she recalled the unsuccessful attempts as child trying to convince her father to make the small tool shed in the back yard a stall for a horse. She recalled and acknowledged to her credit the attempt to pose a cogent argument by going to the library and doing research on Shetland ponies. She memorized their height and weight to present to her father as a lucrative alternative for the small yard size and shed size. Neither plan worked out as it was a child's vision of an impractical and strictly residential neighborhood. Try convincing her thought of zoning laws.

"Let's go to The Baguette," suggested Luke. He knew that would make Rudi happy. She loved the location, outdoor dining and bread. "That sounds great; can we talk a few minutes though about leaving South Florida?"

They had many discussions about their life in South Florida, feeling like an island without family and yearning for something more fulfilling. Neither had lived in a setting outside of a rural town. The pace of South Florida was not what they were accustomed too.

With careers in perpetual motion, Rudi had put off having children and Luke was in full agreement on the decision. Luke did not fight Rudi on the conversation but did not ingratiate her either. He knew that if you gave Rudi a ball, she would run with it. He loved her passion and zeal for life but took it as his role to bridle her energy. Not smothering or controlling "but bridle it somewhat.

It is a strange unforeseen series of events that lead Rudi and Luke to Brown Hill Farm. It started this Saturday morning when they went for breakfast at a local restaurant.

Rudi pulled Luke away from the entrance to the restaurant and towards the kennels of Greyhounds at the make shift adoption site set up by the local adopt a Greyhound charity.

Rudi learned about the fate of the Greyhounds while living in Florida. Most Floridians are used to seeing the adoption programs on the weekends at malls and retail shops. Although Rudi did not become actively involved in the pursuit of saving Greyhounds she remained committed to her belief that no animal should suffer a death once their profitability diminished her and Luke never adopted a Greyhound but showed interest and donated money to the cause.

As Rudi pet the dogs, she was asked if they were interested in adopting. Rudi replied, "No thank you but we will donate money. It is so upsetting to me what happens to these beautiful animals, I applaud your cause."

The lady asked Rudi if she was from Pittsburgh. "No," replied Rudi. "Close enough though, Columbus, Ohio." It was a common practice of transplanted people to attempt to decipher accents and dialects. Rudi was guilty of asking people where they were from once hearing them speak. "My husband is from Latrobe, Pennsylvania though," admitted Rudi.

The lady became so excited that she proclaimed she in fact was from a neighboring town. She moved away from Rudi and pulled Luke over to the side. Rudi laughed to herself because this is just the sort of unproductive banter that Luke despises.

After allowing Luke to suffer enough, Rudi grabbed his hand and proclaimed that she was starving. The Greyhound lady was not so willing to release the couple.

She turned to Rudi and asked her if she was involved with the Greyhound adoption program and Rudi told her "no." They lived in a development and felt that they did not have room. It was the standard response to such a question. One question lead to another and Rudi had informed the lady that she and her husband were looking to move back north and have property where they can house dogs and horses.

No sooner did Rudi finish her statement but the lady moved even closer to the couple and grabbed their hands. "Oh gracious, I cannot believe it! My sister just viewed The Old Bauchmann farm, it is going up for sale. It is in Everstown, Pennsylvania. It's an old horse farm. You know you can rescue a retired racehorse. They slaughter them just the same as Greyhounds." She rambled on stringing sentence-to-sentence failing to view the expression on Rudi's face once she mentioned that racehorses suffer the same fate as the Greyhounds. The lady was consumed with gossiping about the family that lived there, the wife dying years ago and the husband dying soon after. The remaining children fought over the property and it fell into disrepair. Etc, etc, etc. Rudi and Luke learned the entire neighborhood gossip within 5 minutes. The lady then ran behind her table and wrote down a name, number and address, ripped it from the binder and shoved it in Luke's hand. "You must call my sister if you are really interested in moving back up north. Go look at this property before anyone else does. It is not on the market something about some floorboards needing replaced. I know Lois will show it to you if I ask her. The family will not get around to fixing the house up and making it ready to show officially for at least a month if not more." The lady was so excited Rudi and Luke could hardly follow her.

"This was fate Luke. Call Lois, tell her Elaine gave you the number." Rudi begged as she struggled to dig through her purse to find their cell phone. "I will Lois, in the meantime, and tell her about you two." As she spoke she reached out and grabbed Rudi pulling her to her in gesture to hug her. Rudi did not have time to respond or react. She went along with an ingratiating hug then pushed the stranger back and turned towards Luke. The lady stepped towards Luke and he sensed what was coming, so he stepped forward to hug the lady in return. "Thank you for the help," replied Luke.

"Thank you so much, I hope this works out," said Rudi. The two grabbed hands turned their backs and laughed to each other.

"Wow," said Luke. "That was nuts."

"I know but oh my God, this is great," Rudi burst out with uncontained excitement.

The two entered the restaurant and Rudi could talk of nothing else, she bubbled over with excitement. There was even more motivation than normal within Rudi. She was determined to view this property, buy it and rescue a needy racehorse although she knew nothing about horses, the town or the farm. Rudi continued to bring the subject up to Luke although he was attempting to read the menu and deviate from the subject.

"What do you think?"

"About the eggs Benedict?" replied Luke with the intent of teasing Rudi?

She did not get the joke; she moved right over the sentence and replied, "NO, this farm. Should we go look at it? These are the types of deals that end up working? Don't you think?" Luke did not reply as he knew she was not finished, he thought he would just retain his comments until she had made her sales pitch. He did not look up. He continued to scan the menu. "Luke, this is really important to me, what do you think?" Luke put down the menu and looked over at Rudi.

"I know that you are excited. I know how you get. I know this important to you Rudi, but in all honestly I am not all that crazy about restoring some ole piece of abandoned beat down shit hole. Do you know how much money and time it will take? What about our house here? Where would we live while the house was being renovated? There are a lot of issues and stumbling blocks with this type of venture Rudi. We will continue to discuss it but I am not as excited about this as you are Rudi. And racehorses, what do we know about horses? We don't even have a dog or a cat. Hell, sweetheart, we don't even own a hamster." Luke retained his composure as Rudi overflowed with vivacity. He was more levelheaded than Rudi. She knew however that she had a green light. This was just his way of telling her that money was an issue with this venture.

Rudi was not one to dwell on negatives. When she gets convinced that something is right, no matter how insurmountable she cannot be redirected. "Luke, I really want to look into this. At least make the call to the lady and find out more about the property. What is there to lose with that?" Rudi was trivializing her intents at this point. She had already saw, purchased and moved into the abandoned farm that she just learned of.

At this point Rudi decided that it was in her best interest to leave the subject. If she pressed the subject longer she may not leave on a positive note. The waiter appeared and Rudi spoke up, "I am ready to order. I will have the eggs Benedict". They both looked at each other and laughed. The waiter did not understand the tacit joke but smiled and took their order.

As soon as they arrived home Rudi phoned the realtor. She read from the business card given to her from the Greyhound lady. The realtor's voicemail answered. Rudi left a long detailed message about how she had just met her sister and how she was told of the property. "My husband and I are very interested in viewing the Old Bauchmann Farm. Your sister told us all about it and it sounds exactly what we are looking for." When she disconnected the call she laughed at herself resounding Luke's chastising words as if he was there. "You sounded way too excited," she imagined him telling her. She was aware that she sounded exuberant but could not contain her excitement for the sake of downplaying the potential sale to the realtor. After the voicemail, she sat at her computer to start researching racehorses, racetracks, and the fate of the horses but more importantly her new life. After some general research she learned that horses suffer the same ill fate as the racing canines. She drew the strange parallel about the woman who rescued Greyhounds could possibly help her achieve her goal to rescue racehorses by putting her in touch with her sister, who was the realtor for a farm. A farm back north where she wanted to move. It was so serendipity.

Luke entered the room with a cup of coffee for Rudi. "I am going to sit out by the pool. Why don't you come out when you are done planning the rest of our life?" He said as he placed the coffee on the table and kissed her forehead.

"You wait Luke Hudson, you will love it, and you will be Farmer Green Jeans!" They both laughed and Luke left the room.

CHAPTER SEVEN

The Call

Rudi could not sleep that night. For some unknown reason she felt compelled to look into the strange clandestine property that the Greyhound lady spoke about. Tossing and turning that night she lay awake thinking about her life, Luke's life and the possibility of a new start on a farm in Pennsylvania. She was not happy with the busy professional life that they were leading. She wanted more. Her and Luke was not planning a family as of yet. They had both been consumed with their individual careers. Family was not a part of their day-to-day lives. That saddened Rudi. She longed for more. As she lay awake she thought of the farm. It was a place waiting for her to breathe life back into. She thought, "It is a place where I and Luke can start a family, make plans and fulfill dreams."

She loved Luke more than her words could describe. When they met she knew at the moment they exchanged glances that this was her soul mate. Their relationship had not always been perfect but she loved Luke with all of her soul and she knew he reciprocated.

They were merely surviving and moving in peripheral directions at the moment. She wished more than anything to change their relationship to a more solid, meaningful and family rooted

She mapped out her game plan. In the morning she would call about this property. She and Luke already discussed it. He was agreeable to her ambitious plans. She could not wait until day broke when she could call about the property that she felt compelled to investigate.

As she fell asleep, her dreams were of first love. The time when you first see the other person who makes your heart jump and your pulse soar. The feeling of first sight, breath and feeling of love. She dreamt of a strange property and the feelings of first love and the excitement of the unknown fills your being. She dreamt of a long driveway and at the end, a farmhouse stood, tall and majestic. Suddenly she saw an axe and a vision of a man, maybe Luke, striking her over and over again. She awoke in a sweat. Shook off the nightmare and tried to recapture the first moments of the dream that felt so right to her.

The next morning arrived with the sound of her cell phone ringing. She sat up and leapt out of bed. This is the day she thought.

Rudi called the number of the lady who was the contact to the farm. The lady was merely a real estate agent. She did not know the history of the farm or the people that lived there. She informed Rudi that the house was in a derelict state and in an estate battle with the children. "Sad and strange," thought Rudi. "Why don't the surviving children want to live there?"

She arranged for the agent to meet them at the property in one week's time. She was comfortable with the time frame. She needed time to organize plane tickets and travel arrangements. No one was viewing the property as it was in a state that was unfit to view to the public. It was not safe apparently to walk through. Rudi felt lucky to have the first view of the property and saw the situation as perfect.

She called Luke from her office the minute she hung up from the agent. "Luke, you will not believe this, I am so excited." Luke was conditioned to Rudi's over exaggerated enthusiasm. "Tell me what is up sweetheart."

"I spoke with the real estate agent showing or going to show the farm. It is not on the market yet due to some structural issues. I guess there are some ceilings or floors missing."

Luke laughed to himself thinking, "What am I getting into?"

"We will have the option to view it because the Greyhound lady is sisters with the agent. Isn't that great?"

Luke replied, "It is great Rudi, I cannot wait." He was intentionally sarcastic to stir indignation within Rudi.

"Luke! This is so cool. I cannot believe that you are not as excited as I am!"

"Rudi, I am, I am just fucking with you!" They both laughed and agreed that she would make the necessary travel plans.

CHAPTER EIGHT

Unsettled Homestead

The flight was uneventful. Rudi and Luke spoke of their vision of the farm and what they hoped they would find. Luke did not have high expectations however Rudi had a full image in her head of what the property would look like. They had not seen pictures of the property. The realtor merely described the property. Rudi was under the clear impression that Lois did not want to send pictures for fear of driving them away.

Rudi and Luke navigated to the property with the directions given to them from Lois. It seemed very easy to find. As they turned onto the road where the property was addressed, Rudi had difficulty containing her excitement and stress. "This is stressful!" She blurted out to Luke.

"Yeah, about as stressful as going shopping with you Rudi." He knew this was the beginning of the end. He was fully aware that she would love the property regardless of the condition and that they would throw endless amounts of hard earned savings into renovations. "There, that must be it," Rudi pointed to a long stone driveway that had been overgrown with weeds and brush.

Luke turned slowly on to the drive. He bottomed out the bottom of the car as he turned and descended. The stones had been washed away and the road was eroded with large potholes. "Ah, note to file Rudi, we have not even gotten 10 feet onto the property and already there is repair work, like: fix the driveway so we do not ruin the cars." Rudi ignored the comment. Luke did not mean to incite her, he was just having fun. Rudi was too preoccupied with looking beyond the stone drive, scanning the parameter for a view of the house that was described to be beautiful with large white Georgian columns. When Rudi and Luke drove down the stone driveway to view the property that they had flown across the country to see, they were not anticipating or expecting a particular, anticipated outcome. The long steep driveway was overcrowded by weeds and brush. The stone was worn in spots and the muddy ground was pushing its way to the surface.

As they drove down the drive the house appeared out of the weeds to the left of the drive. The house was secondary to the overpowering sudden appearance of the large, gray, weathered structure, the barn., At first glance of the property, there were clusters of images to register. Brush and overgrown trees, garbage, abandoned cars and tall grass, empty beer cans, garbage bags, rusty car parts all took possession of the yard. The imposing structure stood tall and proud over the littered landscape with whitish gray weathered wood that looked like a black and white photograph from the past. Luke stopped the car and turned it off. Neither spoke. Rudi opened the door and got out. She stood without moving as if mesmerized, staring at the barn. "It is beautiful," she said.

"Beautiful? Are we looking at the same property? I can think of many adjectives Rudi, beautiful is not one of them." Luke replied. Rudi turned around where her feet stood. She did not notice that the wind had picked up and a cold damp rain came across the farm.

"Let's go into the barn to get out of rain while we wait for Lois," suggested Rudi.

As they opened the rusty latch to the barn wind pushed rain into their vision. The door was a traditional split entry barn door. The top and bottom door had separate latches. The top half of the door did not have a latch so as the wind picked up; it banged against the frail frame of the door. Luke struggled to open the bottom and finally gave in, "Let's just go to the top of the barn where the door was ajar." They both ran to the top part of the barn that was level with a ramp that met the large sliding doors.

Once inside, they both looked around with wonder. Regardless of what either thought of the house, property or surroundings, the barn was amazing. "This barn is unreal, isn't it?" said Rudi.

"It is really cool," replied Luke. As they stood gazing at the large hand cut timbers that flanked the ceiling they were interrupted by Lois.

"Hello?" She sheepishly entered the barn with a flashlight beam scanning the floor. "Oh, there you are, I saw the car and assumed you were in here. The rain is miserable. Hello, I am Lois." she held out her hand.

Rudi held out hers, "I am Rudi and this is my husband Luke." All exchanged pleasant greetings.

"Well, this is a long way to travel to see a farm."

"Yes it is, but we are very excited to be the first to view it."

Luke squeezed Rudi's hand this was their silent communication, this gesture meant; let me do the talking. "We came up here to visit family anyway, we thought we would also view the farm." Replied Luke before Rudi could avoid the "hand squeeze".

Rudi gave Luke a confused glare shaking her head in confusion. "What is he talking about?" thought Rudi to herself. Then it dawned on her, he was trying to appear as an uninterested buyer.

"Oh, you have family here?" Lois looked amazed. They really did not. Rudi's parents were in Ohio and Luke's parents were deceased.

Luke replied, "We have family in the area. So, let's see the house." The three left the barn and headed towards the house. Rudi glanced down at the ground and noticed an old path had been beaten down where they walked. "This must have been the path from the barn to the house," she said out loud.

"Yes, it must have. A family lived here for many years, farming this land," commented Lois. "The parents died years ago and the two children fought over the property until now, for some reason they decided to sell it."

"That is sad, commented Rudi. "Why didn't one of them want to live here?"

"I do not know," commented Lois. The children probably have their own families and homes by now." Lois did not sound convincing. Rudi and Luke glanced at each other and were now stood on the porch waiting for Lois to find the keys.

As they walked around the house the obvious conclusion was that the house was close to being worthy of demolishing. Rudi however saw a much different image. She saw images, hope, and visions of new floor plans, bright paint and traditional wood moldings. Luke did not quite know what to think. It needed a lot of work. It required money that they did not have at a disposable level. "I do not know Rudi. The place looks like it needs some serious renovations."

"Luke, please just try and not make a snap judgment. This means a lot to me. Just go with it okay?"

As they exited the house, neither was commenting and Lois did not speak. She plotted a game plan to wait until she could gauge their level of interest. It was an awkward moment. Rudi asked if she and Luke could have a minute alone once they descended the house and were back on the small cluttered front porch.

The property was not eerie or haunting, it was unsettling. It was unsettled and lay in a state of abandonment. Unsettled in the appearance of the extemporary esthetics yet the large gray structure of the barn was overpowering and calming. The wood was not falling off and the shutters that covered the window were still hanging. The appearance was just that of a black and white photograph. It was artistic in color variation where the white wash had faded and the gray wood was prominent. The barn was angled on the property so that it stood apart from the other structures. The barn took precedence over the property. There was no fencing left around the pastures. Weeds grew tall and moved rigidly in the fall breeze. Rudi and Luke pulled up around a small turn around and stopped in front of the barn.

"Wow," said Rudi, "this place is amazing." Luke looked over at here He understood her vision and gift for imaging the unimaginable. "We could do this Luke. I feel at home here. I am supposed to be here. I am home."

Luke loved Rudi and knew it would make her happy. It would fulfill her. His instincts nagged at him to talk her out of the purchasing the property, but his heart told him to make his wife happy. "It depends what they will accept. We need to go back to the hotel room and make a list of what needs to be fixed, the cost, deduct that from the price and go from there. I am not making an offer now Rudi. I will tell Lois that we will call her later."

"Okay, I really want this Luke. I cannot lose this property." Pleaded Rudi. "How can you lose something you do not have Rudi?" replied Luke.

"Let's leave and get some distance. We will talk about it." The couple walked over to Lois who was getting out of her car to meet them.

"So, what do you two think? It can be really something special."

"Yes, it can be, but with endless pockets," replied Luke.

"We are both tired. Let us go to the hotel and we will call you tonight." He said.

"That is good, here is my card, and I will write my home number on the back, call me."

She handed the card to Luke and shook their hands. She got into her car and pulled out her cell phone. They could not hear her conversation but imagined that she was calling the owners.

The rain and wind had stopped. The weather encouraged exploration. Rudi was not ready to leave. "Let's stay and look around."

"Rudi, the realtor is gone, that may not be a good idea to be here without her." Rudi was already heading back towards the barn. She noticed the large sandstones that formed the base of barn. "Aren't these old stones great?" She was running her hand along the rough hand cut stones. When she got to the corner stone she noticed letters carved into the stone. "Look Luke, someone carved their name in here." "Noah" "Bonnie" "Pete". "Wow, I wonder who they are. Do you think they lived here at one time?" The letters appeared to be written by children. Some letters were larger than others and some deeper than others. "How old do you think this is?"

Luke headed over to where she was standing to look at the etched stone. "I guess they lived here at one time, I do not know how old it is," Replied Luke.

"Don't you think that the history to an old house is bizarre? I wonder who lived here. Were they happy? What were their lives like?" asked Rudi.

They both paused for a moment and looked at the stones and contemplated the names etched in the large brown earthy stones. "Come on, let's go back to the hotel and eat. I am not comfortable being here without the realtor."

Rudi agreed to leave but only if Luke promised to call the realtor that night and arrange for them to return the next day. He promised and they both got into the car and descended down the driveway. Rudi looked back at the barn and the house as they left knowing in her soul that this was their home.

The two checked into the hotel and made their way to their room without much communication. The both of them were deep within their own thoughts, rehashing the sights of the day and the potentials of the homestead. As Luke opened the door, Rudi walked in before him throwing her purse and duffle bag onto the canopy bed. This was their first stay in the small family owned hotel. Rudi fell back onto the bed with her arms out wide. "I am really tired, how about you?" As she did her eye caught a large box sat on the desk centered in the room. A large pink bow draped over the box. "What is that?" she almost stopped short of falling onto the bed. She sat up, sprang to her feet and moved towards the desk. "I do not know who it is from," replied Luke.

Rudi did not see a card. "I do not know? Should I open it? Maybe it was not meant for this room," stated Rudi.

"I doubt that, open it." replied Luke.

She looked puzzled but found excitement in the unknown package. She opened the large box to find a new brown English riding saddle. She looked at the saddle and searched for a card or a note in the box. On the back of saddle a small brass plaque on the saddle. It read, "To my Rudi, Love Luke"

Rudi's eyes filled with tears and she turned towards Luke. She was utterly shocked and surprised. She fell into his arms and hugged him tight. "How did you send this? When did you send this?"

He admitted to her that he had been to Pennsylvania to visit the farm last week instead of taking the trip to New Jersey as he told her. He asked for forgiveness for the small indiscretion of the truth and laughed. "I met with Lois last week to see if this was going to work for us. As soon as I saw the property Rudi, I knew you would love it. I put hand money down on the property."

Rudi was figuring out the plot and smiling larger than her face could bear. "We already own the farm?" she questioned tentatively. If you hated it I could have gotten my deposit back."

"You hate it don't you? I will call Lois now for a refund," he laughed and moved towards the telephone.

She jumped on him kissing him on the lips. "I cannot believe you, you bastard! You lied to me!" she yelled at him.

"Wow, this is not what I expected," as he threw her on the bed.

Rudi stopped the joking demeanor and looked into his eyes. "I do not know what to say. I love you, I belong there Luke. The saddle means more to me than any other gift you have ever given me." She hugged him tight. He did not comment as he was filled with emotion and did not want to release his tears.

They lay on the bed for a few moments silently exchanging love and appreciation for each other. "How did you know what size saddle I would need?" Rudi commented out of the silence.

"I measured your ass last weekend when you were sleeping."
They both laughed and Rudi got up to inspect her gift. "So,
when you told me that you were in New Jersey, you were viewing
the farm?"

"Yes," admitted Luke.

"I cannot believe you kept this from me! What else are you
hiding? I need to start monitoring your cell phone calls," Rudi
teased him.

"What you do not know will not hurt you my love, besides,
what fun is there to life if there are no surprises," Luke replied.

Rudi wondered silently what wonderful deed she did in her
life to find such a person. She felt calm and at ease as if her life
was developing.

Luke did not need to telephone Lois that night. She had
already had a deposit and was informed in advance that if there
was a red flag he would let her know immediately. Failure to
call equated to everything going as planned. The two of them
had dinner at the hotel and spent the night in the room. Luke
phoned Lois in the morning. He received her voicemail. He was
not surprised as it was Sunday morning.

He left a message. "Lois, as expected Rudi loves the farm.
Please call me today when you receive this message, we would
like to visit the farm before we return to Florida today."

CHAPTER NINE

Unfinished Business

Aces drove through the woods making a swift path to the cabin in an intolerant, inimical mood. He was not impressed to hear that Iron's girlfriend was in fact in the bar and slipped away as Butcher, Luko and Jackal performed their duty under the watchful supervisor of Dempsey. The girl managed to go into the ladies room undetected and slip out the window into the back alley of the bar. The feds had already tracked her down for interrogation. Aces' informant was also tracing her movements. She fled to Texas where her mother lives. This was a costly mistake. This was a witness. A witness who knew an undetermined amount of information about the business of the Skalds. If she were left to testify, many members would go down.

Aces' was determined not to let this happen. He felt a strong responsibility to protect the members and his own freedom. Aces was filled with rage as he made the journey to the cabin

.

As he pulled up to the timber wood porch, Peter heard the guttural muffler that was unmistakably Aces' bike. He looked out of the window peering through the faded bed sheet that served as a curtain. This was an unplanned visit. Aces' plans did not deviate from the onset. He knew from his experience that this was not going to be a social visit.

Aces kicked the kickstand down with the heel of his boot as he pinched the end of his cigarette with one last drag and flicked it onto the ground. He exhaled slowly and threw his leg over the saddle. He removed the bandana from his head and sopped his brow with it. He placed the black head wrap in his back pocket and made his way to the door. Upon reaching the door he did not bother to open it. He kicked the door, hard, with his boot. The door flew open sticking the wall behind it. Peter was prepared and waiting already sitting at the kitchen table with two open beers.

He stood up in an act of respect and held out the opened beer offering it to Aces.

Aces snatched it from Butcher's hand. "You fucked up my friend. You, Luko and Dempsey fucked up. The bitch was in the bar and ran to the bathroom and escaped. Best I know she is in Texas now."

Butcher shook his head in disbelief. He was aware that mistake could take him and the others down. "Fuck," replied Butcher. "How the fuck did the cunt get away? I didn't see her. She must have got away before we got there. There was no one on the barstool beside Iron when I got to him," replied Butcher trying to remedy the situation. "I'm sorry, I will take care of it."

"Sorry, sorry you mother fucker. Is that all you have to say?" Aces was glaring and clenching his fists. He was about to grab Peter by the throat when Peter backed up and said, "I will take care of it. I will go to Texas and find her and finish this."

"Damn straight you will." replied Aces. "You need to shut her the fuck up. The feds now have their fucking nose into this, asking questions and stirring up a lot of shit. We don't need this shit right now Butcher."

"Fuck Luko and Dempsey. This has to be done right this time. You are going with Dempsey." Dempsey was the number two guy in the gang. Dempsey was short for Dempasky, Ron's last name. None of the members used actual last names to protect their identities. Dempsey was as close to the real name that was permitted. In any discussions public or private the gangs appointed names were the only names allowed to be used. Deviation of this rule could mean expulsion from the gang. Expulsion was rarely getting "thrown out". Peter did not get along with him, nobody got along with him. Aces appointed Dempsey as his number two a few years ago. Everyone went along with it because his father was respected as a leader decades ago. He knew what to do, when to do it and finished his jobs. He was in charge of distribution of cocaine. He had a stellar track record for catching up with delinquent clients. "He is coming by to go over the details with you. He should be here in awhile."

Aces allowed his stature to relax some. He sat on the chair and lifted the beer to his lips. He took off his black leather jacket and turned it around to display the large red and white logo that was hand painted on the back. "See this, this is your life. We were here for you when no one else was Butcher. I am your fucking mother, father, brother and wife. You take care of this so I don't have to take of you. 'Cause you know I will you no good fucking cocksucker. No matter if I want to or not, it is what it is."

He was smiling as he spoke and shook his jacket in Butcher's face. He knew he was not joking although his posture was relaxed. You did not get second chances with the Skalds. The feds had been investigating the gang aggressively for a year now. Money laundering, contract killings, drug distribution and slot machines were high exposure but profitable enterprises. Butcher was in the contract extermination subsidiary. He did not have room for error. This was a massive mistake and he was aware of the necessity to remedy it.

Aces grabbed his jacket and rummaged through the pockets. Inside the zippered pocket he pulled out a large bag of white powder. He tossed it at Butcher. "Here, I brought dinner." Butcher caught the bag as before it hit is face. He opened the bag and cut four large lines on the table. He did not ask Aces if he wanted a line. Aces would not have brought out the bag if he did not want to use it. Butcher had a debit card and rolled up single on the table. The two of them talked, drank and snorted, passing time until Dempsey showed up.

The sound of an approaching bike halted their interactions. Aces stopped speaking turning his head like a hawk waiting for approaching prey. He stood up and went to the window. He peered out to see Dempsey approaching. "Dempsey just got here. We can get this going." He went to the door and opened it. Both Aces and Butcher stepped out of the cabin and onto the wood porch. They stood waiting for Dempsey to approach.

Butcher dreaded this next few hours. Aces entire personality and relationship with him would change. It would become him verses the two of them. Butcher was on the outside scratching and ass kissing to get in.

Dempsey walked onto the porch swearing that he stepped in mud, scrapping his boots on the porch steps he yelled, "What kind of shit is this? I hate coming to this fucking shack." He stepped up to the porch and held out his arms to hug Aces. "Hey man. How's it goin'?" he hugged Aces briefly and perfunctorily and Aces exchanged the cold sentiment.

Butcher held out his arms, good to see you man." Dempsey gave him a cold hug and replied, "Ok you fucking bitch, let's get you out of this."

The three of them went back inside the cabin. "It's fucking depressing in here," Dempsey said. "You like it don't you Butcher? It reminds you of that shack you grew up in."

"Fuck you Dempsey. At least I had a shack, you grew up in a fucking tin can."

The banter was harmless. There were six more lines cut on the table. Dempsey sat down and re rolled the single before being offered. He pushed his hair back off his face, bent down and snorted the larger of the lines. "Okay, enough bullshit, let's talk."

Dempsey goes on to update them. "This skank is living is some tin can with her whore mother in some redneck fucking trailer park in Texas. She already gave the whole story to the feds. Last word is that they know the Skalds did the hit and they will use her as states witness. She needs to go, before this gets any further."

Aces spoke up as he sensed that Dempsey was overpowering and usurping his authority as the leader. "Fucking hold your dick Dempsey. My informant didn't tell me any of this shit. Where are you gettin' it and why the fuck ain't I gettin' it?" His motivation was to put Dempsey back into his secondary place. By Aces had already been briefed by his informant and was fully aware of the severity, risks and posturing of the feds. Aces had a management style of portraying himself innocently in an effort to obtain information from his men. He always assumed the position of laying back and letting them hang themselves.

"I don't fucking know Aces'. I am just relaying what I was told. Go the fuck to Luko, Jackal or Butcher if you want to chew someone's ass out." Dempsey got the message and changed his tone minimally.

"The feds are all over this New York job. The only way to stop this from snowballing anymore is to end it."

Aces spoke up, "Enough! I'll fucking fix this and you will listen to me. You two are taking a little southern comfort trip to Texas. Find the cunt and finish her like her cock sucking boyfriend. I do not want you to drive. Take a plane. We cannot lose any more time here. No one else is to know about this, understand?" The two shook their heads.

"I trust you two will correct this fuck up. If anyone goes down for this I will see to it that you both take it up the ass."

Butcher spoke up with a rare dose of confidence in front of Dempsey. "I promise on my word this will be done." He held up his beer bottle to toast. "Fuck that Butcher," replied Dempsey derailing his competency, "I won't come back if it is not taken care of."

He did not hesitate, he hit bottle to bottle with Aces. Butcher once again acquiesced to the third slot. They all agreed and abandon the subject. The three finished solidifying the details. They drank beer and snorted coke until the bag was gone. Aces passed out, Butcher followed too closely to know who passed out first.

Dempsey left the cabin once the two passed out. Walking out into the darkness with a clear head and vision of what needed to be done to protect the integrity of the members. He sat on his bike and lit a cigarette. Smoke filled the dark swirling around his head. When the cigarette was finished he drove off down narrow path away from the cabin.

CHAPTER TEN

Fighting Into Place

The jagged branch reached out and wrapped around Rudi's legs and arms in combat for survival. They have staked their claim on Brown Hill Farm and battled to own it. Rudi spent long endless days restoring the fields and pastures. Often driven to tears from sheer physical exhaustion and pain from cuts, scratches and bruises. She was determined to bring her vision to reality. She found it disrespectful to all that sowed the land and labored before her that it was in such a state of disrepair. The sun had moved over to the west side of the property and the air was growing colder. This was nature's time clock for ending the day. Rudi stood up and stretched her back by placing her hands on her hips and arching backwards. She sighed loudly. "Another day," she said out loud. Luke did not participate in the manual labor that Rudi partook in. He was working longer days than usual trying to settle into the transfer and his newly appointed territory. Rudi had taken her vacation time before her actual resignation as she was due several weeks of paid vacation and wanted to utilize it.

She glanced at her work and felt a sense of accomplishment uncommon to her paying job. There was something very satisfying about restoring their farm. She felt as if every step breathed life back into the old property.

She looked over at the huge pile of branches, weeds and jagged brush. She learned from one of her neighbors that the jagged brush was called "The Living Fence" by the local farmers that planted them. The formal name for the unruly bushes was Multiflora Rose. They were brought over to the area by the local farmers that traveled to other states, for the purpose of making property borders and fences from their thorny branches. Little did the farmers of that time know that the birds would transplant the seeds and the wind would pollinate the thorny brush to unwanted areas. Soon the local farms and woods became overpopulated with the spiked bushes and eventually overpopulated the farmland. Rudi sarcastically laughed out loud each time she engaged in hand-to-hand combat with one of the plants. "I win," she would triumphantly announce each time she ripped one out by its roots."

Rudi was waiting for Luke to return home from work. She glanced up every other moment to see if she could see his car entering the drive. They were meant to drive down to the track that afternoon. Rudi had made arrangements to visit the stables and speak with some of the owners who have horses to sale, for horsemeat. She announced herself as a person who was looking for a horse as a pet. She was met with suspicious doubt, which she did not yet understand. She did not know what to expect so she did not have any preconceived images in her head. She was also doubtful that they would find one today. It was actually too early. The barn and paddock was not ready nor was the fencing up.

As she immersed herself back into the task at hand she heard the sound of rocks crushing under the weight of Luke's car. She looked up and brushed the hair out of her eyes. "Thank God! I need a break," she said to herself. She got up, straightened out her back, grabbed the rake, loppers and handsaw and headed towards the house.

She entered the house yelling up the stairs to Luke. "Just a minute and we can go!" She quickly changed and met Luke out by the car.

The trip to the racetrack was long and boring. Little scenery paved the landscape. As the two of them drove through the barren steel mill town, the rusted black sooty buildings spoke of a time when the town once thrived. The track was off in the distance and Rudi asked Luke what he thought they would find.

"By the look of this town Rudi, I imagine we will find old horses with no teeth and sagging backs with 90 year jockeys riding them around a dirt track." They both exchanged laughter and Rudi admitted that she was not really prepared for the event. "I have no idea what to expect." They were both uneducated with the affairs of a racetrack. It was no secret that is served as a treadmill environment where animals with such grace and beauty were mere commodities.

The back stables where the horses are kept were lined in rows with patched steel, wood and plastic covering spotted holes in the roof. The handlers were thin and pale. They look lifeless as they walked the overly spirited animals. "It looks like the animals soak up all their energy doesn't it?" commented Rudi. She looked through her scheduler for the stable block number where she was to meet her contact, Gail. An older woman who played a political role at the stables. There in the corner. Rudi pointed to stall along the end.

Horses were being walked to and from the racetrack with jockeys perched upon their backs. Some horses where being walked by another handler on a horse side by side. Horses were whinnying and anxious. Handlers were rough and unfriendly. The two parked the car and got out. Neither knew where to walk, on which side…They apologized to every other horse for being in the way. Rudi and Luke were dressed as if the just arrived from a day shopping. Both stood out awkwardly. As they made their way to the stable they walked into the stable. The stalls were dark and small. Cats littered the dirt pathway. The horses stuck their heads out through metal gates as if they were prisoners in a cellblock. Rudi walked up to one, as she held out her hand it pinned its ears back and bite the air towards her fingers. "Okay, not liking you," commented Rudi out loud. Luke stood back in the doorway as if he was safer at that distance. As she walked over to the neighboring stall an older woman with large baggy Levis and green rubber muck boots appears. She had a flannel shirt unbuttoned with a yellow faded long john shirt underneath. Her nails were long and caked with mud. Her gray hair looked like a horses tail pulled back loosely off her face. "You must be Rudi. I'm Gail. Nice to meet you." She held out her hand that was dirty and frail. Rudi grabbed it and shook it, not wanting to appear snobbish.

"Yes, you must be Gail. Nice to meet you. Hiding over in the corner is my husband Luke," she pointed over to where Luke was waving his hand.

"Hello," he replied.

"I was hoping I had the right stable block. Wow, this place is not what I expected." After she let the comment out of her thoughts through her mouth she realized how demeaning it sounded. "It is a different world here for sure," replied the old horsewoman. What are you looking for? I have two that I am done runnin. They aren't doin' much and the owner wants to let em go. Can't afford to keep them here if they're not winnin'."
"

She walked over towards the end stall. "That is sad," announced Rudi as if she was not there to serve as ambassador of goodwill, "But I understand the concept of racing these animals. We are from South Florida where Greyhound racing is huge. Floridians actively adopt them."

"Well people round here don't actively adopt these. Too much trouble, expense and time." Rudi and Gail reached the end stall and the horse inside stood at the end against the wall. It did not approach them. "Here Billy," Gail made a loud clicking sound with her mouth. The horse did not move. "He is old, nice, but old."

"Is it a he?" questioned Rudi.

"Yes, it is a gelding. Most round here are. I don't recommend looking at a stallion if I were you. You will have your hands full enough with a racehorse let alone a stallion."

Gail opened the stall door, you can go in," she said to Rudi. Rudi walked through the gate slowly and timidly. The horse did not move. His head was hung low and his eyes blinking shut. She noticed his big beautiful brown eyelashes. He was large and grayish black...The gray fur looked as if he had aged and became gray. She held out her hand and spoke softly to the horse. "Hello Billy." "Shh. It's alright." He allowed her to stroke his forehead. She actually felt as if she was welling up with tears. The horse had no life in him. There was little to no bedding, the walls were solid wood with pieces of horse hairs splintered through it. He stood with one back leg bent up with his hoof perched. She noticed small white dots scattered throughout his fur. He smelled of old urine and had stains of urine and manure on his side. Rudi leaned in to view the uniform white dots. "Maybe it's powder?" As she stared at the objects they appeared to move, or maybe they were so small against the large animal that her vision was blurring. She leaned in closer and it became evident to her logical thinking that the dots were bot eggs and they could be moving. She tried to figure out the cause. "The horse had not been groomed in so long and the condition of the stall was damp and dirty. He had bot eggs all over his body!" It made her skin itch and she turned away quickly as if to run from the stall pretending she did not see the repulsive condition in which this poor animal was being kept.

Rudi turned and walked out. She needed some air and some light. Gail had turned and was speaking with Luke. She exited the stall and latched the door. She could not stop a tear from falling from her eye. She quickly brushed it away so that she did not appear immature or overly sensitive.

She cleared her throat and spoke up, "How old is Billy?" The old cadger replied, "10, 11 maybe, I am not sure anymore." He has not run in a long time. I like him though and haven't had the heart to get rid of him."

Rudi replied, "Let me think about him. Didn't you say that you had a red one?"

"Didn't you like Billy Willy?" commented the old lady. Rudi found the rhyming sentiment cute. She chuckled to herself. The dichotomy at this place, she looked all business, hard luck and hard done to, yet she makes up rhyming names for the horses.

"No, I like him very much. I just wanted to see both." The truth is that Rudi would have loved to take him, and the red one and the gray one. How do I choose one when they are all needy? Two horses was pushing her time frame, remodeling budget and upkeep budget. She did not want to make any irrational decisions at this time. "After I see the red one I will decide."

Gail was walking out of the barn with a limp from a bowed leg. She hobbled as she moved. "Java," is in my friends stable next door. She headed out with Luke and Rudi turned to look at the horse in the stall. She looked for a moment and his head bowed a few times as if he was acknowledging and dismissing her from tormenting herself. She did not speak to the horse again. As she walked out she noticed another horse sticking its head out of the stall swaying it frantically from side to side and calling out. The horse beside it was chewing the top of the stall door and bobbing its head up and down. The mood was crazed and insane as if they were all screaming out to her at once for help, or attention, or comfort. She turned quickly and ran to catch up with the two that were already heading down the corridor of activity.

"Here we are. Java," she called out and clicked her tongue against her teeth. This time a horse stuck its head out immediately. The horse was perky and bright eyed. His coat was shiny and smooth. He had a large white blaze down the middle of his forehead.

"This is Java," He reminded me of a cup of coffee once you add milk. "He is a bright one. Not a good runner though, can't get him to go in the gate."

Rudi walked over to the horse feeling rejuvenated from the last experience. She held out her hand and called his name, "Java, aren't you beautiful." He stepped forward, startling Rudi, she stepped back away from the stall, as she did he lifted his upper lip showing his teeth. They all laughed at the humor in the moment.

"Why is he doing that?" asked Rudi.

"Oh this one is Mr. Personality," replied Gail. "He thinks he's human, actually I sometimes think he's human." Rudi went to open the stall and Gail stopped her. She reached over to the tack area and grabbed a tattered old red nylon halter. "Here, put this on him before you go in."

Rudi had no idea how to put the halter on. She picked it up and looked at it. Luke looked at her and asked Gail a question as to move the focus away from her. He knew she had no idea how to halter the horse.

Rudi panicked for a minute and held up the halter. She thought to herself, "This has to go over the head, so then this over the nose," she was figuring out the locks, buckles and clasps.

She walked into the stall holding the halter high and in place as if the horse would simply walk into it. Java looked at her and turned his head the opposite direction. She walked over to his head and spoke out loud to him, "Please help me out here so I don't look like a complete idiot." Java looked at her as if to say, "Okay, but just this once. There was this intractable laughing look in his eyes. She allowed her to place the halter on his head.

As Rudi led him over to the stall door she overheard Luke asking her if he had any health issues. "He bowed his left tendon a year ago but it has not reoccurred. But as you know once you bow a tendon it can be fragile." Luke just looked at her as if he had no clue what she was saying. He did not pretend as Rudi did. "What is a bowed tendon? You mean a tendon as in muscle to bone in the leg?"

"Yep. Horses that are young or race before their developed often pull that muscle. When they do, it bows out and swells. You have to wrap it and sweat it, it's crappy."

Luke laughed to himself as she described the injury as "crappy".

"I bet," he commented to her.

"Bring him out Rudi," called Gail. "Walk him around." Rudi had never handled a horse before. She was scared, trying to look as if she was not; she was ignorant as the handling of the creature although she was trying to appear confident.

Java walked with her, nudging at her back with his nose. Luke found the entire scene amusing. Rudi walked the horse out of the stall and into the corridor immediately outside of the stalls but still within the stable. There was not way she was going to walk the horse out into the outer corridor where all the handlers and jockeys were mounting, dismounting and parading horses in and out.

"He is beautiful. Here Luke hold the lead while I look at him from behind." Luke walked over and held the lead speaking softly to Java. "Play the part and you may get a new home," he said. Rudi walked around the horse looking him over. Gail was going over the feet, the ankles and knees. She reviewed all the features with Rudi and commented that he had no injuries or foot problems.

"How much do you want for him?" asked Rudi.

"What the KILLER would pay, $700.00."

Rudi could not believe the nonchalant attitude in which she said the KILLER referring to the payment of death for this amazing creature. Rudi spent $700.00 on a pair of shoes.

"I'll take him," she announced in a burst of self-assurance.

Luke spoke up, "We will?"

"Yes, we will. Can you hold him for a week or two until I can get the fence up?" Rudi asked Gail.

Gail thought for a moment and said, "Yes. We can arrange for hauling him unless you are comin' back with your trailer."

Trailer, thought Rudi. "No, can you please transport him?"

"Yep, for a fee."

Now Luke spoke up, "How much?"

"$75.00," said Gail. "Besides, I want to see his new home". She had a rough demeanor but you could see the love she had for the animals in her hand movements as she stroked the mane and back of the horse. Her rough weathered hands became graceful and loving. She patted Java on the side and said, "you're a good ole' boy, you hit the jackpot here JJ."

Rudi laughed and asked why she called him JJ. "His race name is Java Java." She walked over the front and pulled his top lip up and back. She revealed a tattoo. It appeared to be numbers. He is a registered thoroughbred. "Here is his registration tattoo." Java was not impressed. He breathed out blowing mucus from his nose hitting her in the face. She pushed his nose aside and yelled lovingly at him, "Don't snot on me."

Rudi had settled down and was appearing more at ease with the lingo, handling and tense movement of the stable rows. As she asked Luke to give Gail the deposit and exchange numbers as she walked Java back into his stall. "It's you and me Java. I have no idea what I am doing but you are coming home to Brown Hill Farm," she looked into his eyes. "I promise I will always take care of you and never let anyone hurt you." She gently kissed the young horse on the whitish fur on the tip of his nose. He looked at her and blinked. She felt his eyes communicate with her. A tear filled her eye and she removed his halter. She forced herself to turn and exit the stall comforted with the knowledge that she would see him again soon. As she walked out of the stall, Java stood head on watching her leave. Rudi had saved her first horse. She never owned a horse and Java in four years was never valued as a companion.

She could not abandon the vision of the older gray horse. She called over to Luke. "Luke can we speak for a minute?"

He replied, "Yes," and walked over leaving the old woman in the corridor. "I can't leave that gray horse here in this condition. He has bot eggs all over him, the stall is dark, damp and gross." She was too emotional to find a better adjective.

"What the fuck are bot eggs?" he replied.

"Focus Luke, that is not what is important now, I want to take both but want to run it by you first."

"Since when did you need to run anything by me first? If we agree to settle with two that is it. Then we need to get out here before you adopt the whole friggin' track."

She turned triumphantly and proudly announced, "We will take Billy and Java." Gail was delighted and smiled replying, "They're both great boys." Rudi and Luke headed for the car. As soon as they were seated inside Rudi placed her head in her hands leaned over and began to cry. Luke reached over to rub her shoulders. "It's alright sweetheart," he stroked her back. He knew she would respond to the sights and conditions of the stables and horses in this manner. "You saved two. That's something isn't it?"

She stopped sobbing for the minute and opened the glove compartment for a napkin. She rubbed it on her nose and face. "Yes, it's a lot. I just wish that I could do more."

Luke suggests that they leave. "I think we should go, I don't think that this environment is helping you at this point." The two walked to the parking lot. As they did, a strong breeze swept through the tunnel that led to the track. The wind echoed through the tunnel and the sound of the horses pounding the sandy soil thundered and drowned out the peripheral noises. Rudi looked out toward the end of the tunnel and onto the track. The horses running, their manes moving to the current of the wind. They looked like a pack of wild horses running free. Yet they would return to their small dark stalls at the end of the run and wait until they can run again. Sadly stifling their natural spirit.

They reached the end of the tunnel and turned to the parking lot. As she approached their car the sound, the wind died. Rudi opened the door and sat still in the seat looking ahead but not focusing. Luke put the car in reverse and the figure of the shanty-like stables grew smaller and faded into the background as if they disappeared. Rudi thought driving away was in a sense an act of ignorant abandonment. As if the entire culture, the people, the horses, were ignored. They came out of deprived living conditions all shiny with brightly clothed jockeys sat proudly upon them, all for show. All as fleeting and minute as the time it took the large graceful animals to make their way around the track. Running desperately to meet the poverty that was waiting for them on the other side. "Ignorance is not bliss," commented Rudi out of the blue as they made the journey back home. She was already making the list of preparations that she would need to start early the next day to prepare for her new additions.

CHAPTER ELEVEN

Lying Lambs

At times Rudi's vision of how the farm should look was so far ahead of reality that she felt she would not catch up with herself. She was running a personal marathon against her own goals and visions. She had new motivation this day. She was working against the clock to bring Java and Billy home. As she tired, she thought of him pacing the small dark stall. It made her sad and provided her with motivation to hasten the paces to renovate the barn and stalls.

Once again the light of the day was turning gray and the air was chilling her back as she tried her best to wrestle the Multiflora brush that overtook the paddock. Rudi had finished the surrounding property and had now moved to the barn and surrounding ground before clearing anymore of the unkempt property.

The paddock was not just overgrown with brush it was littered with broken glass, rusty mechanical parts and old tires. She stood in the paddock pitching garbage into a wheelbarrow and hauling it to a rented dumpster. She reached down to pick up broken glass and the sharp piece cut through her glove into her palm. She felt the cut and saw blood soak through her glove. She was too fatigued to call out for Luke; she stood up and threw the glass and gloves to the ground. She felt as if the farm had a force that was competing against her to leave the barn overgrown and derelict. The cut she suffered felt as an intentional blow intended to call a stoppage to her work. Which it did. She had laid a bottle of water and a towel just inside the lower part of the barn earlier that day. She walked over the split barn door tightly holding the cut.

It was not lit enough to see in directly inform of her yet dark enough to find herself stumbling. As she entered the barn from the opposite side of the split-level doors. She was unfamiliar with this part of the barn. She had thoroughly explored the barn as of yet. She only knew of the one entrance that she stumbled upon when she and Luke first viewed the property. She felt that part of the barn was a comfort zone. The architectural structure of the barn was curious to Rudi. It was build into a hillside. Where she just entered was considered the "lower level" that faced the paddock. The barn was known as a bank barn. She learned that the early farmers in the area would build the barns into the side of a hill so that in the summer the part of the barn that was built into the hillside would stay cool and in the winter it would serve as insulation and keep the animals housed inside warm. This side of the barn was dark, damp and moldy. Spider webs were as thick as fog. Rudi decided to take this unknown route as it would be quicker to the front of the barn than walking all the way around and through the overgrown brush. She slide open the rusted door that sat on a channel above and below the door. The door slide open barely enough for her to squeeze through. Once inside she began to navigate in the dark through empty desolate stalls.

She walked about ten yards and tripped. The surface of the ground felt soft as if she stumbled on a piece of rug remnant. Rug remnants, "that would not surprise me," she thought, "There is everything else littered on this farm." She stopped to open the shutter windows that ran along the side of the stalls facing the paddock where she had been working. As she opened the window she noticed she was standing on fur. She knelt down to feel the ground and touched a small round object. She picked it up innocently to see it better in the light barely visible at this time through the window. As she held it up it became visible. It was a small skull. Sickened and horrified she dropped it and ran out of the barn. She did not quite know why she was running but she felt her senses on edge as she imagined bugs and maggots crawling on her skin. Once in the house she frantically began washing her hands, arms and face. Luke heard her moans and came to her.

"What's up? He asked.

"Get the flashlight, there is a skull in the barn."

"A what?" replied Luke.

"A fucking skull, please Luke, get the flashlight!" She did not wait to dry off her arms and face. She opened the door and ushered Luke to the dark stall.

Once in the stall Luke shown the light on the spot where Rudi said she dropped the skull. As the narrow tunnel of light shown on the ground, brownish fur with white spots was decomposed on the ground. It you looked close enough you could see the figure was small, maybe 2-3 feet. The figure was curled up like a lamb. The legs were still intact.

"Shit, it's a fawn", said Luke. Rudi did not speak; she stood a foot or so back trying to make sense of the figure.

"A what? Baby deer?" replied Rudi.

"Yes, it is fawn. It must have been born in here and died somehow."

"Why in this stall? There were three other stalls closer to the wooded area? How did the mother get into this stall? The door was closed when I came in," said Rudi.

"I don't know Rudi. It is dark and I cannot really make heads or tails of this. Let's leave this until morning and I will come out and dispose of it." Luke sensed that the decomposed fawn deeply disturbed Rudi. He had to admit to himself that it did make logical sense. He did not want to make the matter worse though. He downplayed the scene and grabbed Rudi's hand. "Come on. Let's leave this until morning."

Rudi was tired, defeated and unnerved. She did not dispute Luke's request. She took his hand and walked back to the house. All the while feeling disturbed and confused. Why that stall? Why was the fawn laying in that position? How old was it?

She went into the house and ran a bath to soak away the day's fatigue. As she went to bed that night she could not get the sight of the fawn's skull with patches of fur still attached to it out of her head. The position of the fawn was so calm and innocent. Like a sleeping lamb in the field. She could not reason how the death of such a small animal could look so peaceful.

She recalled all the death that they have encountered during the brief tenure at this farm. The fawn, the death of her kitten only days after they moved in, the dead birds that must have flown into the windows of the house. She tried to shrug off the feeling that this was not a good omen. She was determined to remain positive that this move and this farm were right. She could not ignore the multitudes of small deaths that have occurred. She was aware that farms and farmers view death differently that people who make animals pets and immortalize them. She hoped that she would not grow harden to death of animals whether domesticated or wild. The small fragile body of a bird or a fawn, or her kitten. All the deaths seemed to center around undeveloped or young animals.

That night she dreamed of all the animals that she found, loved, viewed or cared for. All were buried in a large field.

There were hundreds of gravestones with names of all of her pets since childhood, all the animals she attempted to care for throughout her life, and the animals she came into contact with that died. As she walked through the Pet Cemetery, they all cried to her. She began to run toward the entrance to the cemetery. When she exited through the gate, she was standing in the barn. In the stall where she found the fawn. The stall was filled with red paint. A bucket of red paint lay in the corner. There was not brush though. A man was painting the floor of the stall red, he was not familiar. He was using a small woolen cap, dipping it in a rusty metal paint can and mopping it on the floor of the stall. As he lifted the cap out of the can it dripped with thick, deep red paint. He would smear the paint on the floor with the sopping hat. He did not stop; he did not look up at Rudi. She turned and walked out of the barn. She was walking back to the house but the house in the dream was not the farmhouse. She was walking back to a small shack. It was a small one-room cabin.

Rudi awoke and lay there analyzing the events and scenes of the strange indecipherable dream. Exhausted, she slipped back into sleep, this time, without dreaming or remembering the dream.

CHAPTER TWELVE

Deed In The Dead Of Night

Rudi was tired from work and did not have the energy to complete her nightly chores this evening. Luke understood as he also felt the drain of their schedule. They moved to this farm to bring meaning to what they defined as their futile lives, but it was tiring. Maintaining their work schedules, the horses, the renovations, clearing the property was taking its toll on their energy. It was weighing on him more so than Rudi. This was her vision and dream, not his. He found relaxation with whisky on the rocks as his nightly tonic. He kissed her on the lips, turned over and finished his drink. He fell asleep that night with the TV still on. He was fully aware that if Rudi awoke and saw the TV on, and his glass on the night table, she would chastise him in the morning.

Rudi tossed in her sleep until finally opening her eyes and succumbing to the reality that the television was on. She looked over at Luke and swore at him, "Fuck Luke, I hate when you leave the TV on!" She rummaged for the remote and turned off the TV. She laid her head back down on the pillow and tried to find the thoughts that she awoke too. What was I dreaming about? She talked herself into dreaming about her and Luke when they first met. When life was simple and their love was new. As she started to fall back into sleep she heard a strange sound. She sat up thinking that she had not turned off the TV. She began looking for the remote then realized that the television was dark. Luke was sleeping soundly and the room was solid black with the night sky. She sat up concentrating on the sound. She tried to stop breathing for a moment not sure if the sound was inside the house or out.

"What is it? Where is it? It sounds like it is outside." She could only define the obstreperous sound as metal on stone or clay. It sounded like a shovel. The sound was so piercing that it poked through the silent night like a pin through silk. She got out of bed and walked to the window. She could not see anything. She walked to other window that faced the north side of the property, the barn.

"What kind of shitty neighbor is digging at this time of night? Red necks," thought Rudi. "It is 4:00 AM. What are they doing?" She could see through the north window and the moon was full this night. She could not see anything through the screen on the outside of the window. She opened the window to find the sound grew stronger. She strained to see where the sound was coming from. It was not far enough away to be neighbor. It was on their property.

She looked out at the barn see if she could see or hear Java moving. The air was quiet and barn was still. She heard the noise again and followed the sound with her eyes. She squinted to focus on a shadow. She saw movement in the distance.

She could see a figure to the far left of the paddock. It was a man. A man shoveling! His back was to her and he was digging. He was digging a hole. Joe was digging a large hole. "Why is there a stranger digging a hole on my property?" She felt a sick feeling in her stomach and dizzy in the head. Is he going to break in and kill us?

She stood unable to move. At that moment when she thought such a bizarre thought, the man stopped digging turned his head and caught her staring at him. She turned without thinking and ran back to the bed. "Luke! Wake up! Come on, wake up!" Luke stirred and awoke.

"What? What is it Rudi?" He sat up not fully conscious. "There is a man digging a hole, a burial hole on the property, just off the paddock." She grabbed his arm and pulled him up from the bed. As they arrived at the far window the sound had stopped and there was not figure evident to neither her nor Luke. "Rudi, I do not see anything. What did you see? Maybe you were sleeping or dreaming?"

"Luke, I am not senile. I am not losing my mind. I heard what I heard and saw what I saw. I know this sounds crazy but there was a man digging a hole in the woods!"

Luke hugged her and urged her back to bed. "You are tired, overworked and stressed out. Your last business trip is tomorrow and I am sure your mind is on overload." Luke comforted her back to bed. Rudi began to doubt herself. What she saw as absolutely crazy.

"After tomorrow's trip you will officially be a stay at home mom, to Java that is!" She calmed herself and dismissed the incident as a dream. She returned to replaying the thoughts that comforted her into sleep.

CHAPTER THIRTEEN

The Last Trip

Rudi stirred early the next morning, which was actually only hours from when she fell back to sleep after the strange experience, to the music of Luke's cell phone. They had agreed that he would drive her to the airport and pick her up as this was the last business trip of her career.

"What time is it?" she called to Luke who was already out of bed.

"4:00 AM and time for you to get out of bed." Luke replied.

Rudi was anxious to complete this last trip. She felt it was a final chapter to a part of her life that consumed her for the last decade and now at the farm she was starting a new chapter of a new life.

The morning rush hour was filled with cars all speeding and stopping for the same short distance as the crawled to the city. Luke and Rudi updated each other on the business at hand and the repairs of the farm.

"I am going to have to go out of town for one night next week. They want me to go to a meeting with one of the new hospitals in Ohio. You can manage for one night can't you?"

Rudi had never stayed on the large property alone yet. "I guess so," she replied. She was hesitant. The nightmare the night before left her uneasy. "I'm a big girl now. I have to get use to it.

It is our new home." She tried to convince herself that worrying about nightmares was foolish and juvenile.

"The nightmare I had last night was so bizarre. I swear I saw someone digging behind the barn. Strangely enough it seemed so real. You know how the soil here is so rocky and nothing but clay. It sounded just like that." She was pensive as she spoke about the vision.

"You were digging the day before. You probably just had that thought in your head and dreamt about it. You know how that goes." Luke tried to pacify her.

"Did you ever wonder who lived at the farm before?" she asked.

"Yeah sometimes, all houses have that kind of history." He replied. "Yeah, but our house is over 100 years old. That is a little different from the ones in Florida that are 5. How much history can you have in five years?" she questioned Luke.

"Well, you can have some rich spoiled woman sleeping with the pool guy in the cabana house while the plastic surgeon husband who is banging his nurse and walks in on them."

He laughed. "That is history." Luke was referring to their neighbors in Florida.

"Ha, I guess. I was thinking more of how it was like to live there in the depression? Farming the land for means of survival. I found this picture in the barn with some old dairy invoices. I guess the family that lived here had dairy cows and sold the milk to a local dairy store. This picture was of a family, in the yard. I assume it was the Father, Mother, older brother, sister and younger brother. It looked like it could have been winter. Christmas maybe. They were all dressed up. They were stood at an old fence off of the barn. There was a horse in the pasture. Remind me to show it to you." Rudi was thinking of where she placed the picture as she spoke to Luke about it.

"Wow, sounds strange. A family, at Christmas, getting their picture taken. Imagine that."

"You are such a smart ass at times Luke Hudson!"

They reached the airport and Rudi collected her things. Luke got out of the car to walk around and see her off. "Have a safe trip. I love you and call me from the airport or when you get to Houston."

He kissed her on the lips and hugged her.

"Love you too," she replied. "See you this evening." She replied and walked into the terminal.

Once inside she checked in and opened the morning paper. She sat at the gate watching the people that would be on her flight. She wondered which ones would be on the same return flight. As she scanned the faces and stereotyped their professions. "I hope there are no delays and I can finish this day without incident," she said to herself with inspiration and hope.

Luke got back into the car and started the engine. He placed the car in drive and started to move when he had to stop abruptly. A rough-looking man crossed directly in front of him. He looked at the pedestrian with frustration and waited for him to get out of the roadway. As the man stepped up onto the sidewalk another man of similar stature and dress quickly stepped into the walkway. He turned his head and gave Luke a look as if to say out loud, "Wait asshole!" Luke placed his foot back onto the brakes and said out loud for no one to hear, "Is there some dirtball convention in Orlando for bikers? Cross already for God's sake." He looked to the left to see if this was a procession. There was not one else. He placed the car back into drive and stepped on the gas.

As he accelerated he saw the figure of a small boy in a white tee shirt run across the road as if to catch up with the last biker character. All he noticed was white. The boy may have had white pants on also. Luke slammed on his brakes screeching to a stop. The car behind him had also started and stopped inches short of hitting him from behind.

The man in car behind him pressed horn and shouted out at Luke, "What's your fucking problem?" Luke into the rear view mirror to see if he had been hit but was more concerned with the child that he assumed he hit. He felt sick and dizzy as he exited the car to look in front of him. The car behind him sped around him honking the horn.

"Can't you see I hit a pedestrian?" yelled Luke in response to the man's aggression.

As Luke sprang out of the car and to the front bumper he was afraid to view the results. He was sure he would see the young boy mangled underneath the tire. He swept over his brow with his hand to wipe the sweat that was building on his forehead.

He looked down, there was no boy. There was no blood. He looked up at the curb. There was no child. Luke looked confused yet relieved. He looked onto the curb 20 feet ahead.

There was not child but the travelers on the sidewalk had stopped and were looking at him. He noticed a lady looking at him speaking to her husband with judgmental eyes. He noticed the two bikers, they were now side by side entering the building just within sight still.

Luke could not believe that there was no child. There was no accident. He realized that he was still standing in the middle of the road in front of his car with the motor still running. There was a pile up of cars and angry travelers speeding around him.

He shook his head and got back into his car. He sat for another second attempting to contain his composure. He placed the car in drive, looked to the left, the right and the left again.

There was nothing in front of him or in his panoramic view. He pressed the gas and slowly drove off.

"That was fucking crazy. I am seeing things." He reasoned to himself that it was because of Rudi's crazy stories of seeing strangers digging in the night and finding strange pictures of past dwellers. He knew he saw a boy run across the road out of nowhere dressed in white. He could not convince himself that it was imagined. Just as Rudi could not convince herself that the visions she had been seeing were not real.

CHAPTER FOURTEEN

Hit or Miss

It was late or early for that matter as Butcher tried to squint to see the clock on the faded display screen of the small microwave that sat in the corner of the cabin. As the display came into view he read the clock, 4:00 AM. He had a habit of waking up at this hour especially when staying at the cabin. His nose was running and he had to piss. He sat up and slid his legs from the bed to the floor. He leaned over and placed his head between his legs. Shook his head a few times and flung his long black hair over his head to his back. He reached down and grabbed the old black hair tie to tie his hair back. He struggled to fit the hair into the small band.

He stood up and walked to the toilet. It was not a conventional "bathroom" as there was no door, the shower was in the corner and not encased and the toilet was merely bolted to the linoleum tile floor. He was thankful to have running water so the interiors did not bother him. He recalled the events of the prior evening as best as he could remember. He felt tired and malnourished.

The microwave sounded that his instant coffee was ready. He zipped his fly and stepped into the kitchen opening the microwave. He pulled out the chair and sat down starring into the dark cup of coffee. He picked up the empty white powdered baggy that was left on the table. He turned it inside out and placed it in his mouth. He hoped for a small numbing but felt nothing. His cell phone rang, he looked at the display screen to view the caller, it was Dempsey.

He answered, "Yeah?"

He was filled with anger and resentment today. He was pissed off that he was once again summoned to do more dirt. He paid his dues and wanted to be respected. He was striving for a simple goal, to be respected. He resented Dempsey. Nobody ever did anything for him. There was no father paving the way. He knew Aces longer and was more loyal than any other member yet he was still cleaning up shit.

His tone reflected his resentment. "Are you ready or are you still fucking around in your little cabin in the woods?" He laughed.

"Fuck you," replied Butcher. "I am ready. Where the fuck are you?"

"I am outside you prick, get off your ass and look out the window." Replied Dempsey.

Butcher peered out of the crack between the sheeted window and saw Dempsey in a red pickup truck.

"I'll be right out," He grabbed his wallet, keys and a pack of smokes and headed out onto the porch closing the door behind him.

As he opened the door the truck Dempsey was tapping his thumb nervously to Molly Hatchet on the radio.

"Are you ready and prepared to do this?" asked Dempsey.

"Yeah, I thought we went over this already. I said I was ready." Smugly replied Butcher.

"Here is the address," Dempsey pulled out a folded up napkin. An address was written on it in blue ink. "This is where we find her. We get off the plane, I have a friend picking us up, we drive him to a bar, drop him off, and go the trailer park. Find her, one pop and leave the car."

"Whose car is it?" Asked Butcher.

"You are a stupid fuck aren't you? It's your mothers, who's do you think it is? It's stolen Butcher." Butcher always felt better knowing the answer to a question than afraid to ask one. He merely looked out the window as Dempsey belittled him. He noticed that Dempsey seemed nervous and agitated. More so than him. Dempsey had a way of taking out his fear and insecurities on anyone else that was around him. Butcher was used to feeling uncomfortable. He dealt well with the feeling of being displaced or stressed.

As the two of them drove to the airport little was said. They drove past farms, which reminded Butcher of his childhood. He noticed cattle in pastures and reminisced about Brown Hill Farm.

The trip to the airport was quick. Both men parted once they arrived at the gate. They stayed apart in the waiting area and boarded the plane separately. Dempsey sat two rows in front of Butcher. An older lady sat beside him. She asked him where he was going. He replied home, to visit his mother. She was flattered and talked to him about her son who lived in Texas. He attempted to cut the conversation short but thought it better to entertain her conversation as to not set off a memory of strange rude men on the plane. After she had her say he leaned his head against the window and closed his eyes. He played out the scene that would ensue once in Texas. He would be the marksman. Dempsey was only along to assure that he did not fuck up again. That pissed him off. He glanced ahead to Dempsey who was chatting to the lady sitting beside him. She was a bottle blonde. Laughing and placing her hand on his arm as he spoke to her. Butcher glanced over at the woman beside her, with blue hair, reading glassed and a tote bag that said, "World's Best Grandma".

He shook his head and nodded back off.

Butcher awoke to the captain informing the cabin that they were landing in 20 minutes. He opened his eyes and stretched. Dempsey was looking back at him, motioning to meet outside at the designated spot once they left the plane. The air was hot and damp. The black leather duffel that Butcher was carrying was shifted from hand to hand as it slipped from perspiration from his palms. He looked around taking in the new environment. He had never been to Texas before. "A lot of fucking spicks," he thought to himself. "I could never live here." He noticed a sign from baggage claim and followed the directions.

Upon arriving outside, his shirt was dampened with sweat. His shirtsleeve was damp from mopping his brow. He did not want to stand in one place attempting to spot Dempsey so he slowly walked away from the door he exited towards the outer perimeter of the building. He spotted Dempsey getting into an old red pickup truck.

The pickup truck was indistinguishable. Butcher picked up his pace and headed toward the red battered vehicle. It began to move slowly toward him. Dempsey opened the door and screamed out, "Hey!" The driver called out, "How was flight? Get in." Dempsey jumped in and the driver reached out his hand and grabbed the duffle bag from him throwing it to the back of the cab. Dempsey threw his arm around Butcher's back slapping it. He smiled from cheek to cheek and said, "Let's get going, the rest of the family is waiting, let the soiree begin."

Butcher did not utter a word. He sat on the seat closest to the window. The driver slowly drove away from the terminal cautiously avoiding attention.

Butcher did not know the driver. He was a small, dark haired, Mexican looking kid. He seemed young. Large greenish black tattoos covered his fingers and forearms. He had a tattoo on the side and back of his neck. It looked like a religious figure of a woman. He wore a red and white bandana folded over to look like a headband. He wore the bandana across his forehead. Butcher offered out his hand and said "hello."

The young escort grinned and nodded his head nervously not speaking.

"You stupid fuck, he speaks Mexican." Laughed Dempsey. "No English, right Pepe?"

He continued to laugh. The young driver laughed from confusion as Dempsey looked as if he was being polite.

Butcher looked away and out of the window. Dempsey said to Butcher, "We need to go over this." Butcher was reaching underneath of the glove compartment.

Butcher stuck his hand under the molded console on the truck and skimmed the bottom of the surface for extrusions. His fingers sensed the metal object he was feeling for. As he pulled the gun from its taped harness, down to the floor. His weight shifted to his feet and he noticed he was stepping on something. He reached down to pick it up while holding the gun. The gun was a .38 caliber double automatic Colt. Dempsey reached over and was talking as he attempted to hand him a picture. "This is the one that got away Butcher, look at her, remember her and dispose of this picture before you enter any buildings." Butcher was preoccupied, now fumbling and reaching for the object under the heel of his boot. He was listening to Dempsey but was noticeably distracted. He felt a plastic object under his boot. This was the item he was reaching for, he lifted it up. "There's something else down here," he proclaimed.

He grasped a copper colored figure of a horse rearing up. It was dangling on a leather cowboy tie. The horse figure was made of shiny copper colored plastic. He dangled the horse in front of him and Dempsey. "What the fuck is this?" he spoke out.

The driver looked over and smiled and pointed to the rearview mirror. He pulled the figurine from Butchers grasp and hung it on the rear view mirror and smiled.

Dempsey continued reviewing the directions with Butcher. Butcher was too distracted by the copper horse now dangling as if he was rearing up as the truck drove on the uneven surface. He took the picture from Dempsey and folded it, placing it in his coat pocket all the while gazing at the horse and remembering Coffee. "This is fucked up," he said to himself. In the background, Latin dance music was playing, Dempsey was reviewing the instructions like a drill sergeant and Butcher was mesmerized by the light striking the copper horse that dangled and moved. He thought of Noah. He thought of his unborn son. His mind was preoccupied to be attentive to Dempsey's voice and directives.

"Stick it in your pants!" Butcher looked over at Dempsey. He was confused for a brief second then looked down at the gun in his hand. It seemed like minutes that he was lost in thought over the horse figurine. "One. Got it, ONE to the back of the head Butcher. No more than one and make her hard to identify, understand?" Dempsey was growing annoyed with Butcher's look of confusion.

"Are you fucking paying attention or what Butcher? Get your head out of your ass before I kick it out." Butcher snapped back into seriousness after the tone of Dempsey's last comment. "I get it. We have gone over this. I won't fuck this up." Replied Butcher trying to pacify the intractable doubt that was growing within Dempsey.

Butcher shoved the gun into the front his jeans as he was directed. The driver did not shift his eyes from the road. He hummed to the loud ethnic Latin music playing on the radio.

"This is the most important day of the year for Ms. Iron." Dempsey replied before saying,. "The sad widow must pick up her welfare check, cash it and buy a load of blow to get over the hole that buried her lying fuck of a boyfriend. She must be tired looking over her should by now."

Butcher chuckled. "Does Pepe over there know where to drive us?"

"No, he is dumping us and the truck here. The truck is hot, after we finish, we are going to ditch and hitch. We will see Pepe in the PM."

Butcher looked over at the young driver. He did not know or care how this was orchestrated. The driver's gang name was Hodz. He was a member of a local gang that the SKALDS used on the West coast for methamphetamine and PCP distribution. His gang ran the local lab. Their lab was the largest in the Houston area. Once Dempsey found out that the girl from the bar fled to Houston he informed Aces. Aces contacted the head of the local chapter with certainly that she would be procuring her methamphetamine. Once she was detected the rest was rudimentary arithmetic.

The group pulled into a down-trodden business district adjacent to a low class neighborhood. Butcher noticed children playing on the street. Men sitting on porch steps and aluminum lawn chairs on the porches smoking cigarette and drinking beer for bottles. The sun was low and air moist. All players were of Hispanic origin. As they sat on the porch laughing and drinking with their cheap ribbed tee shirts Butcher observed.

The driver pulled behind a dry cleaner store. The three descended the truck. Two went right one left. Butcher and Dempsey walked around the block and got back into the truck. The keys were left in the ignition. Dempsey and Butcher drove for another 45 minutes to a desolate trailer park. The ground was sandy and dusty. There were no trees, no bushes or landscaping. Butcher was used to the green landscape of his rural western Pennsylvania home. The landscape appeared barren to him. He analogized the trailers were like rusty cans set adjacent in the desert sand.

Butcher did not know if they were at the home of the "mark" or elsewhere. He asked Dempsey, "I need to know the score here, where am I, the dealer or the home?"

Dempsey replied, "They all fucking live in tin cans. The dealer, where you meet the "mark", don't fuck with me Butcher I am in no fucking mood."

"Go into the bathroom and wait. When she enters, you'll know it and what to do."

Dempsey pulled up to the end trailer. The trailer was white, faded and dirty. Two lawn chairs sat abandoned in the front yard. A doghouse sat 10 yards from the chairs with a vacant chain laying in the sandy yard.

As Butcher descended, Dempsey instructed him to do the job and walk to the last trailer on the right. He would meet him there.

Butcher nodded and exited the truck looking at the dangling copper horse as he shut the door. He walked up to the door and entered. He knocked twice as instructed. A medium frame Latin man met him at the door. The man had dark hair tied back in a ponytail. He was wearing a tank top and jean shorts. He was holding a cigarette that was burnt to the filter. He looked old and tired for his young age. His neck was covered with tattoos.

"Butcher?" he called out his own name. The man moved to the side of the open door allowing him to enter. He and Peter did not speak a word. The man pointed in the direction of the bathroom. It was arranged that the "mark" would enter, purchase her meth and be detained. The dealer would instruct her to the bathroom and where Butcher would be waiting.

Butcher proceeded to the bathroom. He stopped in the middle and turned around. He asked the man sitting on the sofa if he had a beer. He pointed to his nose and snorted with a gesture indicating he wanted a complimentary line. The man who answered the door shrugged his shoulders gesturing that he did not understand him. The dealer sitting in the living room looked up and motioned him over to the coffee table where he sat with a woman and two other men. The small room was hot and filled with stale humid air. The men wore tattered white ribbed tank tops and the woman was in a halter top that displayed the large tattoos covering her breasts. The lines were on the table already cut. Butcher looked at the line on the end and bent over to snort it with the straw that lay on the table. He looked up at the man who answered the door with discontent. He thought to himself, "you fucking understood me, you cunt bastard. All you can do is direct me to the fucking bathroom? You spick bastard."

He walked back toward the bathroom pulling his hair back and redoing his ponytail. The hot and humid temperature was affecting his demeanor. He placed his left finger on his left nostril and breathed in hard attempting to gather the residual coke left on his nostrils. He did not look at the hosts again. As he entered the bathroom he removed the gun from his pants. Before he walked through the door to the bathroom, while holding his gun he turned and walked back down the short hall to the coffee table. With his gun in full view he walked over to the lined up coke. He looked at the dealer and without saying a word bent over and did another line.

Butcher was not in his element. He was not on familiar ground. He was not comfortable with Dempsey looking over his shoulder on this job. He needed the extra boost of false confidence. This time he stood up and walked back down the hall and through the bathroom door. The door was flimsy. He worried that he would not fit behind it and the wall. He stood behind the door as best he could. He waited for what seemed to be 30 to 40 minutes. He waited for the moment. He waited for the mark.

He was feeling his pulse in his head when he heard an American voice. It rang out irregular to the Spanish-speaking group. He sat up and attempted to gather his thought.

His thoughts were on Noah and Coffee and Joe. He was thinking of the summer on the farm when he would stand at the fence with Noah watching the young horse run and play in the field. He was close to Noah in a way that most would not notice. Noah looked up and mimicked him as the older brother.

As he jerked from the past and into the bleak reality of the moments that would unfold he strained to hear if the voice was that of a woman.

"2 eight balls."

His mind was rushing and his nerves tense.

"Okay this is it, it has to be her," he said to himself. "Get it together or you'll be fucked."

He held his breath to listen.

The Latino man spoke to the woman in English. "Hello Senorita."

"Can I try before I buy?"

"Yes, you are a good customer."

He heard the woman snort for a second.

He heard nothing, and waited.

"Ah, Senorita, did you hurt yourself?"

"What? Where" she replied.

"You have blood on your face, just here."

"Maybe you should go look and clean it off."

Butcher stood still. Silent. Nervous, tense, cranked. He imaged the woman was touching her face for signs of blood.

"Where is the bathroom?"

"Ah Senorita, down the hall and on the left."

Butcher pulled the slide back the gun and waited behind the door.

The door handle twisted. Opened and a woman entered. She looked into the mirror that hung on the wall to the left of the door.

As she looked into the mirror trying to find the blood on her face that was pointed out by Jesus, Butcher appeared in front of her in the reflection of the mirror. It took her mind a fraction to see the figure that was standing behind her in the small bathroom. She did not have time to respond or time to react.

Butcher held the gun so tight to the back of her head that it pushed her blond hair inward and around the gun. He pulled the trigger. The gun went off removing the her face and placing it upon the medicine chest mirror that stood inches in front of her. Her body slumped to the ground. The gun he was accustomed to using shot two rounds. It performed the job easily and left his signature.

"Fuck you bitch for putting me in this position," he said aloud. "Try to recognize her now." He pulled the gun away, placed it down on his side and walked quickly towards the door. The dealer was already out of the trailer. The door was open and the screen door was swinging back. Peter kicked it open with his foot and walked quickly away from the trailer. He placed the gun in pants and walked down the dusty make shift road to the last trailer on the right.

The red pickup truck was parked to the right side of the trailer. Dempsey was sitting in the driver's seat. Butcher opened the door, got in and Dempsey speed off.

"Did you do it?" asked Dempsey. "She is taken care of," replied Butcher as he wiped his face with the towel from his duffle bag. The two drove to an abandoned office complex, left the truck, the clothes and the bloodied towel. Butcher put on the clothes that he carried in the duffle bag and replaced them with the bloodied ones.

They walked no more than a mile until they reached a ranch. Brahmas stood in the front yard. A small white stucco single story house stood behind the large white cows. The two walked to the garage and opened the door. Inside the small-framed Latino that met them at the airport was waiting.

He was in a small pickup truck with large chrome exhaust pipes and neon running boards. They entered the "pimped" vehicle and the driver hit the remote control to open the garage door.

The three headed back to the airport. A small diner style restaurant was located in a poor desolate neighborhood a mile off of the airport ground. The driver pulled over and into a parking spot, got of the car and walked into the restaurant. The two exited and walked away from the truck toward the terminal. They would walk along the sidewalk that led to the main terminal. Butcher left his duffle bag with the bloodied clothes in the first abandoned truck.

Neither spoke to each other. They arrived at the terminal and waited for the shuttle that would take them to the gate to await their plane. When the bus arrived they were not speaking, tired and focused on concluding the business of the day. The doors of the shuttle bus opened and the two descended the bus toward the terminal. Peter looked at the police offers walking the roads and entrances to the terminal. They did not intimidate him, they evoked feelings of hatred within him. He recalled the local sheriff that investigated Noah's death.

Peter was the first of the two remaining children to descend the stairs that morning. What should have been a trivial daily task became an event of ambiguity. In the kitchen, his mother, father and Sheriff Stowes were talking. When he entered the kitchen they ceased speaking to one another.

Sheriff Stowes just stood in the corner with his hands in his pocket he did not speak nor look directly at Peter. Melinda was sat at the table and Joe was stood on the other side of the room with his hands down to his side in an unnatural, awkward stance.

"Peter, there was terrible accident last night. Sit down." his mother spoke to him in an unnatural, manufactured tone. "There was an accident last night with Noah. He must have been in Coffee's stall and spooked somehow. Coffee trampled him."

Peter did not know what to say or how to react.

"That's not true." he wanted to shout in response but was too afraid of the ramifications.

Peter looked over at the sheriff who did not offer an objection. He realized that the sheriff had obviously bought his father's version of the events. He turned his head and looked at his father with tacit judgment, pain and anger. His father did not look at him; his eyes were focused on the sugar jar that sat in the middle of the kitchen table.

"Dad is this true? Dad?" Joe did not return a reply.

"Is Noah dead? I want to see him. Where is he?" he was not justified with an answer so he continued with his form of interrogation.

"What did you do to Coffee? I want to see him also. I don't believe you." He spoke now with ardor and conviction to discover the truth.

"Peter, I know this a shock. You can't see Noah, or Coffee. We had to put Coffee down." Melinda spoke to her son with artificial conviction.

"I don't want you to remember him like this or ever see such a sight in your lifetime." Melinda spoke with heart and true passion with this statement. "Please do not tell your sister, I will." She got up from the table and walked toward Peter who stood motionless but tense. She pulled him close and hugged him. This was the first sign of comfort and parental contact he had experienced since the previous day.

"Now go upstairs and let us talk." She said as she stepped back. Peter did not want the feeling of her arms surrounding him in comfort and normality to end.

He obeyed the directive and ascended back up the stairs. The events that followed this indelible moment of his young life were motions entangled in a meaningless drama. His father became immortalized for trying to save his young son and killing the horse out of desperation to save him. He was almost a hero for killing the horse. The overinflated masculinity of the neighborhood farmhands would comment that his actions were justified and honorable. Coffee became the undeserving villain.

Peter never questioned his parents nor did he trust authority from this point forth. He no longer trusted anyone with his emotions or feelings. He did not choose to live the life he was living. He told himself that every day. This bitter motivation enabled him to carry out the actions requested of him by the gang he joined. The bikers became his brothers. The leader, his father. The girlfriends his entertainment as no other female figure ever served a purpose of worth. He pledged his love, life and soul to the Skalds after Noah's tragic death.

CHAPTER FIFTEEN

Look For Two

Agent Stinton was preparing to complete his daily paperwork. All Federal Marshal's reported nothing aberrant on the day's assigned flights. He sat at his desk and stretched his arms above his head, looked at his watch and leaned back thinking of the ride home. He was tired anxious to finish his day. The fax machine rang and he turned his chair to look over at the incoming document. He got up and collected the papers that were spooling from the machine and dumping onto the floor.

He read the first page, it was addressed to him. He shuffled the pages and went over to desk to call the sender. It was a friend of his over at the Federal Bureau of Investigations Unit in Houston. He dialed the phone and waited for an answer.

"Tom, Mark here. Got your fax. What's up?"

Agent Carderos replied, "I have a situation that I need some assistance with. Our East Coast division has been following a racketeering, drug trafficking, biker gang that has polluted New York, Pennsylvania and New Jersey. They are into it all but seems manslaughter at a public bar in upstate New York is what they will get them for.

Two of the members have been spotted in a trailer park in your area and without surprise, our witness in the murder charge did not show up at a scheduled briefing."

Mark listened to his friend intently. "You called me because I'm a weekend Harley Hog didn't you?"

"His friend laughed and replied, "Yeah that's right, I figured you had loads of experience with the biker gangs being you ride on the weekend with the other fat old agents."

Mark laughed and changed his tone back to serious, "Which gang are we talking about? Latinos?"

"No, real East Coast grease heads. The SKALDS." They are one of the top five gangs. They used to stay under our radar screen but lately they have been into the bigger and better side of the business. You know they pushed the wops out of the area."

"Yeah, I couldn't handle working with those New York or Pennsylvania interbred fucks." Mark was reviewing the sketches of the men as he spoke.

"I have the sketches, I will distribute them to my men and brief them. I am looking at the manifest for the remaining eastbound flights to the hot bed. There are a few more this evening. I will take care of it. If we see them what do you want us to do?"

"Track their steps, try to photograph and depose any persons they come into contact with and send a report to me in the morning…If they are here on business, they had assistance. I want to know who they speak with, where they go and when they take a piss."

"I'll take care of it. Hey how is Linda and the baby?" he asked his friend with concern.

"She's better. I am glad the birthing ordeal is over. How's Kasey?"

"She is good, getting big and making the old man nervous these days with all the crazies in the world." He replied to his friends jovial questioning.

"Okay, I have to get this organized if I want to shuffle these flights. Take care, Tom."

Mark hung up the telephone and called another agent on his walkie-talkie.

"Stancheck, call the agents in for a briefing and reassignment, ASAP."

Mark collected his papers and walked over to the copier to organize the documents. He left the room in a more subdued mood than when he entered. He said to himself as he walked down the back halls of the terminal toward the briefing room.

"So much for going home at a respectable time. Bikers, never a dull moment in this job."

The briefing room was stuffy and filled with stale air from smoke and lack of air-conditioning. The ten Federal Marshals were summoned to the briefing room hidden in the corridors of the airport were growing impatient.

The metal door opened and the Mark walked in. He was drinking from a bottle of iced tea.

"Gentleman," he called out as a greeting. Mark handed a stack of papers to the nearest agent. "Pass these on." As the agents took one, scanned the text and passed the stack to the next agent, Mark simultaneously spoke to them on the matter at hand.

"I received this memo from the Federal Bureau an hour ago. It seems that they are working on a gang case over in the Eastern Coast. Two of the members that they are following might have done a little work here in Houston today. The Feds received information that an informant is missing, presumed deceased and two of the wanted men were spotted in Palomino

Hills Trailer Park. They requested marshals be placed on planes headed from Houston westbound to New York, Pennsylvania or Ohio. It seems we have three more flights tonight that fit the bill."

The agents listened to Mark as they looked at the sketches of the wanted men.

"The gang is called the Skalds. For those of you who are not familiar with them, or for those of you who do not own Harleys," the men chuckled.

"The Skalds are a deep-rooted biker gang in the Mid Atlantic states, started in Maryland but dominate the Eastern Coast. They have been around since the 1950's. They have upgraded their business to drug trafficking, extortion, for hire hits and petty thefts. They have approximately 500 members in their chapter. The leader of the gang goes by the names of Aces. He is located in the Pittsburgh area. Seems these guys are brazen and have balls, too bad they don't have brains to match. The two that are here entered a bar in New York and killed one of their own members in front of a whole bar of folks. Spilled his brains onto the floor. The girlfriend got out and is here in Houston under Federal watch. She was a local chapter whore. They all know her, quite well I may add.

For those of you who do not know what the word Skald means," (Agent Stinton had a reputation for giving his agents abundant information. His team often teased him for the trivial facts that he knew.)

They were Viking actors and poets who would act of scenes of Viking violence in public forums."

"This is a very violent gang. We are used to the Camacho's here in Texas, but this is the East Coast group. They have over 44 chapters and are about 900 large. Our boys here are the executioners. Or the "Enforcement Team" as they like to call themselves."

"I bet none of you eggheads knew that did you?" he teased the agents.

"We do now and are better off for that little bit of knowledge sir," replied agent Marino humorously.

"What's the girl doing so far from home?" asked Agents Perfett.

"Seems her mother lives in one of our many lovely trailer park communities."

He continued his briefing. "Do not try to approach the men. We want as much information as we can get without tipping them off to change their behavior."

"The best way to ID the one is to look for the tattoo located on his right forearm. It says, 1% in large black and red ink."

"Wait, you are going to tell us what 1% means right?" Called out Agent Marino.

"If you want to know, it stands for the 1% of bikers that are in the gang. Okay, schools out boys."

"Be safe, these men could be armed and are dangerous. Okay, let's assign the last few flights of the evening. I will take the Houston-Pittsburgh flight with Stancheck. Miller and Hopkins you two take the Houston-Cleveland flight. Lucas and Taylor take the Houston-Newark flight. Familiarize yourself with the sketches. If you see them, phone me immediately."

"Men," he called out as the group was dispersing. "You are NOT to speak to them or approach them. We are to mark their steps and make notes of their contacts. Clear?"

The men spoke out in unison that they understood the directive. They got up and departed from the room.

Agent Stancheck walked over to Agent Stinton. "So what's there to do in Pittsburgh?" he smiled and hit Mark's arm. "Not much, football season is over." He replied back to his partner. "So how's Kasey?" asked Stancheck.

The two men walked out of the room and Mark entered a code onto the keypad outside of the briefing room locking the door.

"She is so beautiful and growing up way too fast," he replied. The two men headed off to the boarding area. Mark removed two Starbuck coffee cups from his bag, a magazine and a newspaper. He handed a coffee cup and the newspaper to Stancheck. "Here you go; I get Sports Illustrated this time. I doubt I look believable anymore, I read this paper twelve times today's. We need to get some new props." He pulled the magazine from Stancheck's hands. "How many times have you read this one?" he asked him.

"Oh, about four of five. That is a valuable magazine to me. I can keep using it for the next month to help me pick next year's fantasy football team." Replied Stancheck. The two continued speaking as they made their way to the gate.

CHAPTER SIXTEEN

Crossing Peter

Rudi had successfully finished the business day and managed to catch the first shuttle bus to the main terminal. Her thoughts turned to Java, the Farm and Luke while sitting on the hot, crowded shuttle bus. Rudi noticed two men getting onto the bus. She thought they seemed out of place in the crowd of mid-week business travelers. They were dressed very urban and were not tolerating the Texas heat very well. Traveling was hard for Rudi. She was used to it. She was used to profiling people, she considered it her hobby. As she noticed the two men get onto the bus a man in an undersized, wrinkled blue suit sat down beside her. As he searched frantically in his suit jacket for a handkerchief to swab the sweat from his brow, he found it and wiped his forehead nervously. He politely said hello to Rudi.

She thought her new subject more worthy of a personality profile than the two men that she was previously paying attention to.

Few words other than the typical greetings were exchanged as the bus made its short trip to the terminal. Rudi despised commuter planes but if she wanted to make it home for the weekend she had no choice.

Once in the terminal Rudi sat in the back by herself as usual. Ingratiating conversations from lonely male travelers was one of the hazards of traveling alone for Rudi.

As she sat staring into a cup of diluted diet soda, Rudi noticed that one of the two men she noticed from the shuttle ride had sat beside her. Where was his travel companion? I wonder are they friends, businesses partners? Ah, lovers? No, friends thought Rudi. As he sat down there was a comfortable atmosphere. The two glanced at each other and exchanged smiles. He looked familiar to Rudi although he was rough and someone she would not socialize with. He sat down beside her and she moved to the left away from being overly close to him. As she nudged over she dropped the boarding pass that was serving as her bookmark. He bent over and picked it up handing back to her noticing the destination, Pittsburgh.

"Going to Pittsburgh," he said? Peter did not know why he spoke to her. He was not normally outgoing, especially given the day and the events that had taken place. He spoke to her though.

"Yes, the thriving Mecca of rural Western Pennsylvania. Do you live in Pittsburgh?"

"Yes," he replied. He realized that he was engaging in a conversation that should not be taking place. He did not say another word.

Rudi sensed his trepidation. "I just moved there a few months ago from Miami. I am finding the culture shock hard. My husband and I renovated an old farmhouse. It has been quite an experience." She engaged in the pleasant exchange to cut through the awkwardness of the man's sudden shyness.

He did not reply. He looked at his boarding pass and Rudi sensed that the conversation should be over. She had always made it a policy to not give anyone her name or other personal information. She was disappointed in herself for telling the stranger as much as she did. She slide over to the left a little more and returned to her book.

The two never exchanged names. "Thank God for Prop." she said to herself. It was a shallow attempt to convince her that she did not want to speak with him. The truth was she did. She felt a connection to him. She allowed herself to wonder about the stranger. "It is if I can see into his eyes and into his soul." she thought. "It's like there is this whole other person inside trying to get out." She was so deep in thought that the book slid off of her lap. She snapped back to reality and bent over to pick it up. It had slid to the side away from the stranger. As she bent over she glanced up and he was looking at her. She smiled and said nothing. She picked the book up and leafed clumsily through the pages to find any page. It was irrelevant, she never read the words. She had been traveling with the hardback for the past year. She turned the page, page 70 and she thought to herself, "This is a good page, far enough into the book so it does not look like I am ignoring him." She did not know why she was saying this, she did not want to ignore him. She felt rather out of sorts.

Seconds later the stranger got up and walked over two rows and sat down in an empty seat. "How rude." she thought to herself. "What is deal with him?" She ignored him yet she felt rejected.

She could not stop her mind from dissecting his actions. "Where was his friend? Why did suddenly become so quiet? Why did he get up and move after they had stopped speaking? I thought we sort of had a connection? She corrected herself, not sexual though." She peered over the book to continue watching his actions. She noticed he was shifting the contents of jacket pocket. The stranger removed a clip of money that was aberrant for most travelers. He must have had $1000-$2000, thought Rudi looked back down at her book so she would not be obvious.

After a second she peered back over the top of her book at the man.

Suddenly the call to board the plane was made and Rudi snapped to attention. She stood up and closed the book placing it back in her briefcase. While she moved to the flow of the other travelers shifting nervously to board the plane she glanced back over at the man.

He was no longer seated. She saw a piece of paper in between his seat and the next. "He must have dropped that out of his pocket," she thought. Rudi went over to where he was seated and picked up the paper. It was actually wedged in between the seats. She removed the paper and looked at it. It was a wrinkled photo of a woman and a younger woman sitting on lawn chairs outside of a white aluminum trailer. Rudi felt paranoid, she felt that the other travelers were watching her. She quickly folded the photo back up and went back in line. Her eyes scanned the line hoping to see the man and return the photo.

The line moved forward and Rudi was two people from the boarding the plane. She could not continue to search for the man. She would find him once on the plane she concluded. She boarded the plane and found her seat. She was seated on the aisle so finding the man should be easy. She watched the rest of the people as the boarded the plane.

Rudi noticed the man as he ducked under the plane door. He was speaking with the man beside him. She waited to see who it was. "It's that guy again, the one he was with on the shuttle bus!" she was enthralled with the drama of event. "This is so strange. Why didn't they sit together at the gate?" She looked again to assure it was the same man as on the shuttle bus. "It is definitely him, without a doubt. This is so weird," she said to herself. As it happened the two sat two rows in front of Rudi. She watched the two until the rows filled up and she could not longer see that far in front of her. The plane took off and she waited for the moment when the seat belt sign went off. She would return the photo to its rightful owner. "I would never want to lose a picture of someone I cared about," she thought. "He must care about this woman, he would not carry around a picture of her in his pocket." The man beside her interrupted her thought pattern by asking her if she was in Houston on business. "Here we go." she thought. "Time to find my book."

"Yes, I was and you?" she replied.

Twenty minutes into the flight the bell sounded that it was time to return the photo that already took up too much of her time. Rudi left her seat and approached the man. She interrupted him and his travel companion while speaking. I am sorry to interrupt but you left this on the seat at the gate. She extended her hand holding the photo. "I thought you might miss it." The man looked at her, and then to his partner. He stretched out his hand to receive the photo. He did not even look at the picture, he immediately held out his hand with the photo and replied, "This is not mine."

Rudi looked confused. "It has to be—I picked it up from your seat after you got up to board the plane." He laughed and said, "this is someone else's girlfriend not mine. Thank fuck." And the two started to laugh.

Not knowing how to reply, Rudi said, "Ok, I am sorry." She thought the situation strange. This was not the same personality he portrayed to her while they were seated. The situation was very weird to her. "Okay then, I will just go back and sit down." She said to herself, but actually out loud. As she moved back to her seat she noticed several surrounding passengers gazing at her, which always made her uncomfortable.

Feeling extremely unresolved with the entire scene, Rudi began to replay the last hour at the gate. She was positive it was his. Why would be deny it? Why was he alone at the gate? Why did his friend rejoin him? The beverage cart was coming and Rudi left the unanswered questions. She concluded that the events of the day were indeed strange.

The plane ride was uneventful as Rudi would often describe her traveling to Luke. She was hoping he would be outside of the baggage claim. She hated having to stand outside while a cavalcade of cars drove around time after time prohibited from stopping.

Rudi was off the plane and quickly walking down the hall to the main terminal when she heard her someone attempting to gain her attention. Not as Rudi but, Madame. How she knew it was her was ironic she though as she turned around. Two men escorted her away from the center of the corridor and back to the gate. What now she thought to herself. She was smiling and asked, "I do not want to go backwards here gentlemen, and I am trying to go home, the other way back down the hall." Neither man replied to her. She thought okay? What is going on?

While back at the empty gate, one of the two men asked for the picture. "What picture?" replied Rudi. "The picture that you attempted to give the passenger in row 15A."

"Oh, that picture. Let me find it. Why?" The second man handed Rudi a business card. As he did he asked her if they could have her contact information. "Why?" stated Rudi. As she read the white business card:

Mark Stinton
Office of Homeland Security
Federal Building
222 Congress Street
Houston, TX 23345

"This is so crazy," thought Rudi. She found "A" photo. Her mind replayed the event. She remembered using the photo as a bookmark. "I gave it back to him once I got on the plane." She felt prepared to answer the agent's questions.

"What did they do?" Although she knew she would not receive an answer.

"I am not at liberty to divulge that information to you. I simply need you to tell me what conversation you had with this man." He held out a sketched photo of the shy man that sat beside her. The man who seemed bottled up. The man that did drop the picture.

"I have nothing to do with them; he sat by me and dropped a picture. I picked it up thinking he would want it back. I never met the man. He didn't want the picture back. He stated it was not his."

She began a series of statements that sounded very defensive. They were meant to. She did not need any association with a person being followed by a Marshal.

"Madame we understand, we just want the photo so we can file a report."

"File a report? Report for what?" Rudi thought it but did not want to start a new series of question and answer. "Here it is, and I will give you one of my business cards. If you have any further questions call me, as for now, I am tired and late in meeting my husband. Can I go?"

"I am sorry but I cannot let you leave just yet," he informed her. "I need to take your statement. This will only take an hour or two."

"AN HOUR OR TWO? My husband is waiting for me." Rudi replied with total discontent and frustration.

"Mama me, I understand, we will send someone to greet your husband and inform him that you will be delayed a short while." Marshal Stinton was calm and cryptic.

Rudi reached for her cell phone to call Luke. As she pulled out the cell phone, the Marshal and his partner stepped in. "Mama me we have to take that from you."

Marshal Stinton reached for her cell phone.

"What? What are you talking about? I am going to call my husband." Rudi replied in self-defense.

"Mama me, we cannot allow you to make any calls until we interview you." As he took the cell phone he handed it to his partner. The second Marshal placed the cell phone in a plastic bag that he pulled out of a black carry-on bag.

"We will put your name on the bag and it will be returned to you after we interview you."

The Marshal explained to Rudi as she was escorted down the terminal toward the main terminal. As they reached the bottom of the escalator the Marshal asked her for the make, model and color of her husband's car.

"It a black Volvo. This year's model," she replied without emotion. "You will intercept him from circling the airport looking for me?" she asked.

"Yes, mama me. We will inform the sheriff's that patrol the arrival terminals to look for the car. They will flag him over and inform him that you have been delayed. He will be allowed to park and wait for you." Marshal Stinton explained to her.

"Look, I do not know anything. I am a normal person returning from a business trip," she attempted once again to release herself from the escort and imminent detainment.

"Mama me, please do not speak until we inform you of your rights and record your statement." Marshal Stinton and his companion turned left off of the escalator and walked toward the back hall that was behind the row of escalators. Rudi always wondered where the doors lead. As she walked quickly keeping pace with the Marshal's, she imbibed the surroundings, the secretive doors and hallways of the airport that she was a new witness too.

She could overhear the second Marshal use his radio and call to one of the sheriff's.

"Federal Air Marshal requesting sheriff interception of arrival vehicle. Federal Air Marshal requesting interception of arriving vehicle." He repeated the call twice.

Rudi could only shiver to think of what would happen to Luke and how he would receive the invasion from the sheriff's.

As the three reached the metal door at the end of the hall, Marshal Stinton entered a code into the keypad that was housed where a doorbell would be. The door clicked and he pulled the doorknob toward him. The door opened outward, "After you Mama me," he instructed her.

Once inside the room, he pulled out the metal chair that was placed around a folding table. He asked her to sit and he sat at the other end. There was a television set and a video recorder at the other end of the room.

He pulled out a chair as his partner walked over to the video recorder that was housed on a tripod. "We are going to ask you a series of questions. We are going to tape record your answers. You are not under arrest. We are asking for your cooperation as a citizen of the United States."

"Citizen of the United States? Isn't this a bit melodramatic and overplayed?" Rudi thought to herself. As she was innocent and tired she did not think twice to ask for an attorney.

"We only have a few questions for you regarding the men you approached on the plane." Mark Stinton advised her. "If you answer our questions quickly and honestly this will be short and you can meet you husband and go home. I am sure you are tired." He was obviously patronizing her.

Rudi did not feel it was in her best interest to disagree or become retractable. She was innocent. She did not know the man. She felt that she had nothing to lose by answering the questions.

"Fine, what do you want to know?" She asked.

"First, do we have permission to video record this interview?" He asked.

"If I say NO does that mean you won't?" asked Rudi.

"No, that just means you will sit here and wait for a court stenographer to arrive to make an official record of your statements." He replied.

As she was tired and innocent. She acquiesced and agreed to the videotaping.

"Fine, let's just get on with this please," She replied.

The second agent moved the video recorded closer. Once it was set up on the black "X" that was taped on the linoleum gray floor she turned it on. Rudi was fixated by the movement and red light temporarily. The entire scene appeared surreal to her.

"What is your name and address?" Marshal Stinton asked Rudi.

"Rudi Hudson. H,u,d,s,o,n," she spelled it out with an air of indignation. I live at 909 Canterbury Lane. Westbury, Pennsylvania, 17889."

"What association do you have with the biker gang known as the Skalds?"

"None. I only know of them by what you hear. They ride up and down the roads in gangs. Does it look like I ride on the back of a motorcycle?" she replied smartly.

"Do you know a person who uses the gang name Butcher?"

"No. I have never heard that name before." She replied without hesitation.

"Why did you approach Butcher on the plane?"

"First, I did know his as Butcher or Harry, or Dick. He dropped a picture in the waiting area in Houston. I returned it to him."

"What was the picture of?" He continued his questioning.

"There was a blond haired woman sitting on a chair outside with another woman. I assumed it was his girlfriend or mother so I wanted to give it to him." she explained the events.

The question and answer session continued for approximately 30 minutes. Once the Federal Marshal's determined that she was speaking with veracity, they concluded the questions.

"I want to thank you for your cooperation Ms. Hudson. You have been very patient and helpful. You are free to go. I will escort you back to the terminal." Mark Stinton concluded.

"That's it." Rudi questioned as if she had not had enough. "Don't I get to know what this is all about? Who the hell is Butcher?" she was discontent with the lack of closure.

"You will be contacted by the Federal Bureau of Investigations if there are additional questions or more assistance is required." He replied as he prompted her off her seat.

"FBI. You mean this isn't over?" she asked totally dismissing and overlooking that he had failed to answer her previous questions.

"Yes. This tape will be turned over to the FBI. If they should require additional information from you they will contact you." He was diligent in keeping her moving toward the door to conclude the interview. She was not aware that she was not standing and being pushed toward the direction of the door.

"What was this all about? I deserve an answer!" She demanded again after she realized that her question had been averted.

"Mama me, I cannot divulge that information to you. You have been cooperative and I thank you for that. I unfortunately cannot answer your questions." Mark Stanton again pressed on this time opening the door for her.

Rudi's eyes were dilated and her mind was racing. She had spent 40 minutes or so being questioned in a sterile, florescent light cell. She did not get answers to the numerous questions. She felt disappointed. She felt used. All the while she was not nudged along to where she was walking in a daze back down the hall that lead to the escalator.

She look ahead of her and noticed the entrance, or exit back to the terminal.

The men nodded and pleasantly told her to have a good evening. Rudi mumbled out load as she walked away, "I will."

As she walked out of the back walkway she felt like she awoke from a dream and was slowly entering back into reality from unconsciousness.

The quietness and emptiness of that room, the monotone voices of the Marshal's, the video. As she entered the common area the sound the tram, traveler's voices, movement, motion. It calmed her. She felt soothed as if she was entering the real world again.

The Marshal's nodded at her and she walked away quickly. She got onto the tram. There was another traveler who noticed where she entered from. He was looking at her and she felt uncomfortable. She stared at the floor. "This is crazy, I did not do anything wrong. Why do I feel like a criminal?" she asked herself.

When the doors opened beckoning the arrival of the tram to the baggage claim area, Rudi was the first to exit. She almost ran to the door that led to the outside. As she stepped onto the threshold of the door, the large glass doors slid open. A wave of cool air hit her face and she felt even closer to home.

As she exited she stopped and wondered how she would find Luke. She looked to the left and scanned the benches. He was not there. "Shit, I should have asked them where I would find my husband." She said to herself.

She turned her head to the right and as she did she noticed Luke standing up from the bench where he was seated. A sheriff was standing within 5 feet of him. She saw him inform the sheriff that she was his wife.

The sheriff picked up his radio and spoke into it. He allowed Luke to move toward her and vice versa so he must have communicated with the Marshal's. Both were walking quickly. The movement swept over both of them. They hastened their pace and finally, met. Luke hugged Rudi and she clung to him. "What is going on?" he asked her. "They would not tell me anything. Are you alright?"

"Yes, I am fine. I do not want to talk here. Let's go. I will tell you in the car." She replied. She was so elated to see him that she did not want to reduce the moment with the frustrating recount of the events.

He looked at her and smiled. He was used to the strange comings, goings and happenings of their life. Rudi was an event a moment but this was uncommon even for her. He was happy to see her and happy she was safe. Now that she was in his possession, he would see her home safely. See her safely home to their new home.

Once in the car she told him of the man, the photo and the questioning. "They video recorded me." She stated.

"They what?" he asked again to reaffirm what she had just said.

"They recorded the questions and answers. They said that I would be contacted by the FBI!"

"What the hell did you get involved with Rudi?" he looked over at her as the arm releasing them from the airport parking lot raised up over the car.

"This guy on the plane. He is a biker or a hit man or something. They asked me what I knew about the Skalds." She told Luke.

"The SKALDS, as in the annoying loser biker grease heads that go up and down the highway on the weekends? Those guys?" He asked her.

"What do you know about them? What haven't you told me Rudi?" He asked demonstrating to her that he had not lost his sense of humor. "Are you a secret Skald bitch, whore?"

She could not help but laugh out loud. He grabbed her hand and she gripped back. He pulled her hand up to his lips and kissed her knuckles. "Let's go home. Tell me tomorrow. I bought you a cooked from the bakery today. It's in the glove compartment. There is a bottle of water in the side cup holder. Try to relax for the moment."

She felt calmer. She felt in safe hands. She thanked him and opened up the glove compartment to find three chocolate chip cookies. She opened the package and ate them thinking how good it was to be going home to the farm.

Once back at home she climbed the stairs, undressed and slipped into bed. She did not speak about the events again that night. "Well, I will certainly remember my last business trip." She said out loud to Luke as he got into bed.

"Do other people live like this? I can't even take a business trip without something weird happening!" She told Luke. He smiled and looked at her. "You love not being normal. You wouldn't have it any other way. This may be a little over the top but you know what I mean." He replied to her questions.

"A little less drama might be nice." She replied before closing her eyes. As she did she thought of the stranger at the airport. The man who seemed to reach out to her. She thought about his eyes. Those dark inquisitive eyes. His eyes spoke of his loneliness. She continued to wonder about his disposition. He instigated their conversation, then without cause, something changed his security. He just stopped. He ceased the connection between the two of them yet his eyes emoted the yearning for human interaction.

She was not attracted to him in a sexual way but she could not stop thinking about him.

She wondered if he arrived home safely. Where was home? What did he do? Why was he being watched by the Federal Agents? Her instincts could not be convinced that he was a wanted murderer.

She was egregiously fatigued and mentally drained. As she drifted off to sleep she wondered, about the stranger.

CHAPTER SEVENTEEN

Red Signs

As Rudi entered the barn the surroundings appeared normal. The grass was wet with dew and Billy was vocalizing his discontent over being hungry and first signs of morning were showing through the cracks of the barn wood. This was his sign that it was time to eat.

It was very early this morning. Rudi had a full day and needed to finish the barn no later than 7:00 am.

Rudi filled the coffee cans with feed and opened Billy's stall. As she repeated the task and once in Java's stall, Rudi noticed an empty cellophane wrapper on the floor of his stall. She bent over to pick it up. She found it strange. She read the package and as the words registered in her head she felt unnerved. Rat Poisoning? Oh my God. She turned to look at Java. He was standing in the corner of the stall with his head handing low. She frantically kicked the sawdust bedding around in a desperate effort to find the piece of the bar. She repeated out load over and over again, "Please let me find the poison, please let me find the poison," she repeated the line again as if it would assist her in finding the bar of rat poisoning, she did not. She turned, opened his stall and pulled the metal spring hitch back so hard it sprang shut with a loud reverberation. She ran back to the house to find Luke. She threw open the door and screamed for Luke once inside the house

"Luke I need you in the barn!" screamed Rudi into the quiet house. "Luke!" Luke heard her cry and ran down the stairs. Rudi had already left the house and was running back to the barn. He reached the side door and ran out after Rudi.

"What is wrong?" Luke screamed out.

"Come into the barn, I need you!" Rudi yelled with noticeable panic in her voice. Luke knew something was desperately wrong. Once inside the barn Rudi handed him the empty wrapper of rat poisoning. "How much of this was used? How big was this and where did you leave it?" Having to think what she was talking about, Luke said, "it was an entire bar and I left it in the Tupperware container on the shelf."

"You couldn't have Luke!" cried Rudi. "Java ate it. It was in his stall." Panic overwhelmed the both of them.

"Call the vet Rudi!" Luke was trying to calm his wife. "Go into the house and call him. I will stay out here with the horse." Luke did not know who left the poison out but was overcome with guilt and responsibility. They removed the animals from an unfit life to live out their years on this farm, happily and healthy. He could not comprehend how this would occur. He replayed the events of the night before over in his mind analyzing the placement of things, the placement of the rat poisoning. He was certain he moved it into the secure tack room. He was positive of it. He was last in the barn the prior night. Rudi was inside. She did not come back out to the best of his knowledge.

As he stood in the stall stroking Java's neck, Rudi was frantic in the house. She was able to call the vets cell phone and speak directly with him.

"Dr. Grayson, this is Rudi Hudson. I need for you to come to the farm immediately. I think one of the horses ate a bar of rat poisoning."

"Do you think or know?" asked the calm, almost detached man on the other end.

"I think I know," replied Rudi.

"How long ago?"

"I do not know—Sometime in the night."

"I will be there within the next four hours. The horse may start to bleed out from the compounds in the rat poisoning, it is a blood thinner that causes the animal, preferably the rat, to bleed to death internally."

Rudi choked on the vision of the vets words. She was inconsolable at this time. "Please come sooner. I cannot lose this horse, I cannot witness this. Can't you come now?"

"I am over an hour away in the middle of birthing cows. It will be alright. Keep the horse quiet and I will get there as soon as I can."

The conversation disconnected. This vet was renowned in the area but did not appear overly emotional. She had always assumed it was because of his practice of farm animals. "To leave me here for four hours while my horse bleeds out is fucking ridiculous," she said out loud while stood in the middle of the kitchen.

She left the house and headed back towards the barn. Luke walked out to greet her. "What did he say?"

"He fucking said he would not be here for over four hours. Oh, and I forgot, the horse may die a long slow death by internally bleeding to death." She was crying as she acerbically informed Luke of the possible fate of Java.

"What?" replied Luke. "Rudi, slow down, he moved her over to the step of the barn. "Sit down a minute. Tell me what the vet said."

"Luke, he said that rat poisoning has compounds that thin the blood so that the animal digesting it bleeds to death internally. Tell me, what happens to all that blood? Does it stay inside?"

Luke looked at her with worried emotions. "I do not know Rudi. Let's hope that did not happen. Did you come into the barn after me last night?"

"No, why?" replied Rudi half concerned with his question half not understanding and becoming frustrated with the digression of the questions.

"I have been going over and over this in my head. There was not a full bar of rat poisoning and I swear it was left in the front tack room." Luke calmly replied.

"Do you think someone intentionally came into the barn and poisoned him?" She did not think that was the case but she believed Luke in his recap of the events the prior evening.

"I don't know. I don't know why someone would want to do that? Why? What do we do now?" Luke felt as if the transgression was not leading to a relevant conclusion. He felt that it was highly improbable that someone would intentionally poison a horse that has not been there long. They had not been in the neighborhood long.

"We wait I guess." Rudi got up and walked into the barn. Java was looking tired and lethargic. "I am going to go into the house and get you some coffee and a sedative." Luke had low dose sedatives that he used for work when it became so intense that if affected his sleep. Rudi did not reply. She knew Luke would do as he saw fit regardless if she refused or resisted.

She pulled the stool into the corner of his stall and cried. She looked around the rough hand cut timbers that framed the ceiling and corners of the stall. As she laid her head back onto the wall of the stall she noticed a carving in the wood beam. She leaned over and saw letters. Again, NOA or letters similar to that affect. She noticed more letters that spelled COFE.

She felt the letters with her fingers and wondered about the author. He or she must have sat exactly where she was sitting to have the letters at that level and in that position. "Actually it must have been a child, the letters are lower than an adult position while sitting," she mumbled to herself.

She paused another moment to imagine the barn years ago, then looked up at Java. There was no change in his appearance but it had only been 10 minutes. Luke entered with a cup of water in one hand and a cup of coffee in the other. He placed the coffee down on the ledge of the stall and handed her the water. He reached into his front pocket of his jeans and pulled out a small peach colored pill that was halved.

"Here Rudi, take this. It will relax you so that you do not lose your mind before the vet gets here." She swallowed the pill with the water. She looked up at look from the stool that sat low to the floor and started to cry.

"I cannot believe this. I do not want to see this. I cannot image how much blood there would be in this stall if he bleeds to death."

Luke stood her up and hugged her tightly. "That will not happen." Java walked over and stood beside them as if he understood the conversation was about him. Rudi reached up and stroked his forehead.

"Do you want me to stay with you?" asked Luke.

"No, go about your morning. There is no sense in both of us sitting here. I will call you when the vet gets here and you can come then."

"Okay," replied Luke as he kissed her forehead. "Call me if you need me, I will plan on being back here in three hours." He left the barn and Rudi sat back down on the stool.

Java was standing in the middle of his stall with his head hung low. Rudi placed her head back against the wood wall once again and waited.

She must have dosed off and slumped over allowing her hand to drag on the rubber mat on the floor of the stall. She lifted her hand once she felt the cold wet floor. She opened her eyes and noticed that her feet were placed in a pool of blood. There was blood on her shoes, socks, and pant legs. Her hand was bloody. She stood up and the stool slipped out from underneath her. She slid to the floor falling into the dark red liquid that covered the floor of the stall. She was frantic. She was now covered in red blood. She stood up and looked for Java. He was not there. She pushed her hair out of face but her bloodied hands only made her vision blurrier. The stall appeared bigger? She noticed the figure in the corner. It was a person, crying. She did not know comprehend the scene. She wondered to herself, "Luke, I must have slept through the whole thing and now Java is dead and gone."

She walked over to Luke and reached down, crying, frantic and confused.

The figure was small, too small to be Luke. She rubbed her eyes with her shirt, a spot where there was no blood. As she cleared her vision she noticed the small frame of a boy turning his head to look at her. He was covered in blood and she could not make out his face. It was as if he did not have one. She stood up and stepped back. She stumbled on something on the floor of the stall behind her. She fell again to her butt. She rolled over quickly to her side to see what tripped her. She picked up the object that appeared to be a "twitch" that the vet uses to tie around the horses nose to keep him quiet when administering to him. She picked it up to view it.

It was not a wood twitch. It was a leg of a horse. It was Java's leg. She could see the reddish fur through the blood. She dropped the leg and gasped.

At that moment her head jerked back against the wood smacking the backside of her head hard against the wall.

She looked around. There was no blood. She dreamt it. She looked up at the end of the daylight peering through the front door of the barn as if it were spying.

As she looked up she saw the stranger from the airport. It looked like the man with the dark, deep and sad eyes. He stood at the entrance of the barn just staring at her.

She looked again and the entrance to the barn was empty. She could not place the events of the dream or of reality together. Her experience in the barn with the blood did not feel like a dream. Rudi placed her face into her hands and bent over to her knees. She was tired, frantic and emotional. Then she realized that it was just a dream, Java is still alive. She had never felt relief and hope and thanks for a second chance. She looked up and Java was standing before her. They were nose to nose as his head hung low inches in front hers. "The dream was so realistic that I still feel overwhelmed." She thought as she stood up and walked to the door. She paused, "Are those voices? She asked herself. Still confused and disoriented, Rudi looked out and saw Luke and the veterinarian. They were walking towards the barn.

"Oh my god, this was not a bad dream." She said with fear for her horse.

Luke looked concerned and was still in his work clothes.

The two men entered the barn and Rudi was still dazed. The vet opened the stall door and started asking her questions about his appearance and actions over the last two hours.

"Is that how long it has been?" Rudi asked. Luke looked at her and asked if she was alright. "I must have dozed off. I just woke up."

The vet was not paying attention to her but to Java. He instructed for Luke to get a bucket of hot water and bring it in to the stall with the hose, the jug of oil and set the items on the stool in the corner where Rudi had been seated.

It took Luke minutes to return from the house with the items that were requested and in farm clothes. The vet gave Java a sedative and began inserting the flexible plastic pipe into his mouth. The asked Rudi to hold the end up high and shoved a large white funnel on the end.

He asked for Luke to open the jug of oil and hand it to him. He began slowly pouring the oil into the funnel that feed into Java's stomach. Java did not choke or try to move away. He was swaying and covered in sweat.

Neither Rudi nor Luke spoke to the vet as he worked. "This should help grease the skids," he replied. "We start here and see how it goes." Rudi asked why.

"We need to get his system moving quickly so he passes the substance. If he loses blood it's too late. We can transport him to an equine hospitable but in these cases you find it is too late. If he has not started to bleed out in another hour, he should be fine."

After a few minutes the jug of oil was empty and the vet removed the plastic hoses from his mouth. The vet collected all of his apparatus and left the stall. Rudi and Luke followed. They were both surprised at how rudimentary the procedure was and how open-ended the diagnosis was.

"So that's it?" questioned Rudi. "Yep, you wait." He replied.

"Again you mean?" said Rudi with a tone of frustration. "Unfortunately you do not know when he ate it or even how much he ate. Heck, he may not have even eaten it."

Rudi dug into her pockets to find the empty cellophane wrapper. She could not find it. Annoyed she replied, "This was not a figment of my imagination."

The vet responded, "I am not saying it was, I am saying that there are too many unknowns here."

"I would not do anything outside of what we already did. Call me if he starts to bleed."

At this point the vet was writing his charges on a notepad. He ripped the page off and asked, "Which of you wants this?" Rudi looked at him in shock and disgust. She turned and walked away back towards Java's stall. Once in the barn she looked on the ledge, floor and garbage for the cellophane wrapper. She did not find it. The longer it took to locate the more she doubted herself.

"Am I going crazy? Where is the damn wrapper?" She opened up the door to the tack room and moved items, scanned the shelves and floor. She did not find it.

She turned and walked quickly towards the house. "Maybe I left it in the kitchen when I called the vet," she thought.

Once in the kitchen she opened drawers and went through the garbage. She could not find the wrapper. She checked her pockets once again. She suddenly felt that her efforts were fruitless and unnecessary.

She was overly fatigued at this point. She looked out the window at Luke and the vet as they spoke.

Luke took the paper and relied to the vet, "Wow, $200.00 for a jug of Crisco oil." He laughed with the vet to change the mood of the moment. "I will get my checkbook and be back."

He walked away and the vet continued to load items into the back of his pickup truck fitted with a wooden homemade cab.

Rudi exited the house passing Luke in the yard without speaking to him. She looked dazed. She entered the barn and sat back down too watch Java. For the next twenty-four hours he did not shed a drop of blood. He remained unscathed.

Neither Luke nor Rudi could not rationalize the events that had just transpired. She did not discuss the dream with Luke. The stress and anxiety of the day's events took a toll on both of them. Neither of them wanted to discuss it after it had passed.

As the day ended Rudi thought about it again. "Was there really an empty wrapper? There must have been, how and why would I come up with that?" Rudi felt content in her knowledge that the scene was over and Java was fine. She did not abandon him during the crisis. She felt a connection to him after being so assiduous to his needs. The two of them had formed a new bond. She wondered about the small boy in the stall and all the blood and the horse leg. She wrote the nightmare off as brought on by the sedative and the immense stress.

CHAPTER EIGHTEEN

Second Down

As Peter arrived at the cabin he dismounted his bike in a haze of anger and resentment. A gust of wind swept through the trees removing the last of the winter leaves towards him as beaconing the past. As the leaves swirled and descended to the ground in front of Peter he noticed the leaves and the wind. He stopped. He acknowledged the sounds of the air. It sounded like he heard the whisper of a small voice. "Forgive." The wind sounded the syllables of the words through the trees. He knew he imagined the words. He was tired. He just killed another person. He made a practice of not recounting the fallen obstacles. This job was tiring. Too many, too close in time, too much. He never let go of the anger that slowly ate away his morality. The anger that losing his unborn son was a tariff from the Aces. He did not speak about the resentment. He was not naive enough to think that Aces would offer up any words of inspiration or empathy.

He continued to walk up the steps to the cabin. He pulled a pack of cigarettes out of his pocket and pulled one out. As he lifted the cigarette to his lips his mind reflected on the copper horse that hung, catching and reflecting the light in the truck. He thought of Noah and Coffee and of the summer when he was happy. When Noah opened up and seemed more human to them all. The horse played a role in their lives. It meant communication and belonging to Noah. A source of hope for his father. To Peter, it meant a time when his life had a purpose. He was not in his father's shadow. He was a role model to Noah. Peter's female influences were that of his mother and sister. That summer his sister grew into a teenager. He watched over her with pride and sense of eminence as he protected her as best he could. His mother depended on him. She was not so preoccupied with Noah. Noah was happier, therefore his mother was more attentive to him. He remembered how he picked berries with her that summer. She baked pies and he would air them in the smoke house too cool. The felicity of the summer was short lived. Months later Coffee was dead and Noah was dead. His relationships changed and he moved away from all that he cared about or was caring for.

As he sat down on the wooden kitchen chair opening a beer that he just grabbed from the refrigerator the sound of the wooden legs scrapping on the floor reminded him of the morning that he descended the stairs to sound of the kitchen chairs occupied by his mother, father and sheriff.

Time passed and Peter drowned out the reality of the moment with visions both happy and traumatic. Most importantly, indelible.

He reached for the coffee can that sat on the table. He peeled off the plastic lid and pulled out a small white parcel. He cut himself two lines. One for him. One for his misery.

As he let go to the effects of the drug, he remembered the time he and Noah jumped on Coffees back. The young horse ran around the paddock throwing Peter to the ground. When Noah was lifted onto his back from his brothers leg up, Coffee stood, then walked. Noah squealed with delight. Peter watched Noah that day and did not see his disability. Peter rarely saw the flaws that labeled Noah. He saw an innocence that he wished he had. He thought, "Noah was the lucky one. He did not preoccupy his time with self-induced stress and unrealistic expectations to pacify father." Unfortunately, Peter was tormented and preoccupied with these burdens.

As he thought back he wondered about the farm. He often wondered who bought it after his sister sold it. He did not regret leaving the details to his sister, or never returning for that one last visit. All the while he could not help but wonder if it was destined to remain in ruins or if the new caretakers would restore it to its natural beauty. He refused to take any of the profits from the sale of the house. He felt is he left it and never looked back, he did not want to be a whore to the proceeds. He did not open the letter confirming the sale and providing him with his half of the profits. He sent it back to his sister unopened without a note. That was last he heard from her and of the Brown Hill Farm.

His mind moved from bitterness and back to the farm. He wondered if the new homeowners had children. Were they old, young, happy? Did they feel the immense sorrow, pain and tears that soaked the soil of the farm? He road past once before it was sold. He had just met Aces and was drunk and high. Aces had told him that night that Dempsey was next in line. Peter felt betrayed and once again let down by a father figure. This was his only motivation to drive past the source of his painful existence.

Hours later Peter lifted his heavy emotions off the table to the sound of his cell phone ringing in his pocket.

"I'll be there in five," Aces proclaimed. Butcher got up and walked into the bathroom for a piss. He walked back out zipping his pants then running his hands through his hair.

"What now?" he thought to himself.

As Aces arrived at the cabin he knew that the information he was about to give would not be received congenially.

He walked through the quiet darkness piercing the silence with his boots. He noticed that the air was still and motionless.

The woods were silent. The common sound of the locust was silent. He looked into the cabin through the cracked window of the front door. He could not see Butcher. The stillness was disturbing. His unsettled emotions were no doubt fueled by the knowledge of the cruelty that would be inflicted to Peter over the news he would soon deliver. He would be the instrument that would violate the peaceful silence of the night.

It seemed like hours later that Aces opened the door and walked into the cabin. He found Peter sitting at the table staring off in the distance. There was a look of sadness in his dark, aged eyes. Aces walked over to him and placed his hands on his shoulders from behind him where he sat. Peter went to stand. "Sit down my friend." He pushed Peter back down onto the chair.

"You look like shit my friend," Aces proclaimed.

"You would too if you did two hits in three states in one month." Butcher replied. He intended to be sarcastic and acerbic. He did not care if he insulted Aces at this juncture. He had gotten in over his head. He had taken on more than he bargained for. He was unhappy and mentally tormented. He wanted Aces to be aware of that.

"It seems that you left something in Texas." Peter did not know what he was referring too.

"What did I leave?"

"You left a photo. A photo of the mark, in the airport. It seems a woman returned it to you. A woman who can identify you."

Peter just looked at Aces. His mind sprinted through the events. He was so rushed with adrenaline when he and Dempsey arrived at the airport. He did remember speaking briefly with the woman in the waiting area. He remembered when she boarded the plan she returned the picture of the mark to him.

At the time he wrote the incident off as bad judgment on his part but uneventful.

"Aces, I mean no disrespect but fucking cut to the chase here. I am tired and this is becoming old. I did not sign up to be the sole militia for the Skalds."

Aces sensed his frustration and fatigue. He was not going to overlook this however. "This job has been fucked up from the start Butcher." He answered back with authority and demotion.

"You have not yet finished your work. The girl can ID you and Dempsey for that matter. The feds are all over this job. They have been since the hit in New York. It is not going away yet. You are going to have to get you fucking pussy head out of your ass and finish this."

He reached over and pulled Peter's chair in closer to his. The chair screeched across the floor. Aces leaned over into Peter's face. "Understand one thing Peter. The corners of this puzzle have been placed my friend, but you have one more piece of this puzzle. Unfortunately for you it's damn smack in the middle."

Peter did could not imagine what he was referring to. He would have never in his mind imagine where he was about to be sent.

Aces did not inform Peter of the address. He was fully aware of the address of the witness. His informant told him that she had already been contacted by the Feds. His informant told him the girl was approached by Federal Marshal's getting off of the on the plane. He was also aware that Peter spoke to the girl while seated at the gate before dropping the picture. This was a mistake not commonly made by Peter. Aces felt that there had to be inner influences that lowered his defenses and caused him to become sloppy.

He was approaching the time that he would have to give Peter the news of where the next hit was located. He felt the best way to inform him was to do just that, tell him as a straightforward directive, without emotion or sympathy.

Aces knew that the homecoming to Brown Hill Farm would be wrought with torment. Aces was aware that he would play and integral role in that torment. He led a business. Although the group was an outlaw biker gang, it was run as a corporation. He could not sacrifice the lives of many for one no matter how personal the one was to him. He refuted the personal attachment and handled the matter apathetically.

"Do you have a pen and a piece of paper?" asked Aces.

"What?" replied Peter. The conversation was taking a frustrating turn. More frustrating than Aces premeditated. His taunting and insightful questioning had efficacy.

"You want a pen and piece of paper, what the fuck for?" Peter now was the inquisitor.

"I am going to write the address of the location down." Aces replied without emotion.

Peter did not push Aces. "I am being dressed down for leaving a piece of traceable data behind and he is telling me he is going to write an address down to once again be a risk of being traced, what the fuck?" he asked himself.

He pushed the chair back in an aggressive move and walked over to the table where the microwave sat. He reached to the lower shelf and grabbed a cereal box. He opened the top flap and ripped it off. He grabbed a pencil that lay on the same table. He turned and smacked the box top down in front of Aces. Aces did not rise to Peter's irreverent and obdurate actions.

It was not a secret that Aces was known to the members as a ruthless, violent sociopath.

Aces slowly wrote an address on the box top, set down the pencil and slid the paper over to Peter. He was a coward in reality. He did not have the courage to verbally tell Peter that the woman lived at his childhood farm. He was man enough to give the order to sent Peter to silence her but was not "fatherly" enough to relate honestly to Peter.

Peter looked at the scrap of cardboard. 909 Canterbury Lane. It meant nothing to him. When Peter lived at the farm with his family the address of the farm was a rural route. The post office changed rural routes years ago to aid emergency and ambulance assistance to people living on rural routes.

"You couldn't just tell me this? 909 Canterbury Lane? This is it? Do I eat this now?" he asked with a hint of sedition in his voice.

Aces did not realize that he would not recognize the address. He knew the farm had been sold but was not aware that Peter had no involvement in the transaction. He sat motionless looking into Peter's face. He had an immediate decision to make. Tell him or allow him to discover it himself.

He made the conscious decision to deny Peter from the truth.

"You go to this address when Dempsey calls you. He is scouting the mark now. Once he makes a pattern of her actions he will give you a date. You will go to dumpster behind the industrial park on Route 54. Wait until he calls you. Finish this once and for all."

He was elusive in his directives.

In a sudden outburst unexpected by Aces, Peter blurted out, "fuck this Aces." This was a huge act of indiscretion. He knew it. Aces knew it. The two fell silent. "I have taken on more than I bargained for. I am done. I did this last hit in Houston and now you are telling me that less than 24 mother fucking hours later I have to do another? I am done." He pushed the chair back as it fell to the floor Aces sat still and calm.

He spoke coldly and forcefully. "You fucked this up not me." Aces was pissed off. He loved Butcher as a son but would not accept his irreverence. "You were sloppy. You left a fucking picture. Do you remember that? Jog your fucking coke induced memory. You were sloppy. If you were on top of your game you would have destroyed the picture. You didn't. You are the stupid cunt motherfucker that dropped it in the airport. Get it straight, there is another witness. You and you alone are going to shut up this witness or I cannot protect you."

Peter could not believe what he was hearing. "You cannot protect me? From what?" he asked fueled with rage. He felt betrayed by the man who was supposed to love him like a father. The first father he had let him down and now Aces was following suit. He was disgusted. He was aware that he took the photo from Dempsey. He knew he become distracted by the copper horse that dangled from the rear view mirror. The truth was that he should have destroyed the photo, but he didn't. "Of all the fucking luck," he said to himself. "This one fucking indiscretion that should have gone unnoticed," he spoke to his conscious the benefit of pity.

He spoke up and ended the silent standoff. "Protect me from what Aces?"

"Protect you from violating the code you took when you became a Skald. Do you remember the oath? The rulebook? Your actions have placed others at risk. It is her or you. I cannot and will not tolerate another fuck up Butcher. I cannot continue to cover your ass." There was no misunderstanding the consequences of failure.

"I will do this one last hit Aces but then I am done. I need a rest. If I am getting sloppy someone is to blame other than myself. I am being spread too thin." Butcher replied.

"Boo fucking hoo you snot nosed ungrateful cunt!" Aces snapped back at Butcher.

"You may want to avoid the mirror my son but I will not take ownership of your fucking head games."

Aces stood up and glared at Butcher with a look he had never received by Aces in tenure of their relationship. "I care for you Butcher. Like my son. Don't let me down."

"Dempsey will call you to go over the plan."

He walked to the door, exited and did not look back.

As he walked off the porch he felt the strain of the exchange. The one vital fact was left quietly hidden. He was sending Peter back to do a hit at the place where he experienced great loss and sorrow. No matter how cold and direct his actions were he still felt love for Peter. He felt the imminent inner struggle that Peter would be faced with.

He pulled out his cell phone and called Dempsey. "He is waiting for you now." He hung up the phone. As he started his bike and backed up away from the cabin he could not help but feel that he had let Peter down. He knew he did not do right by him in an effort to make the whole of the gang content. This is something he would have to resolve in his head, in silence.

Peter sat at the table saddened by the exchange and once again feeling betrayed. He could not drown out the sound of Aces bike roar to a start and speed off. The sound remained him of being left. Once again he felt insignificant and disappointed in someone he trusted. Aces bike roaring to a start and fading as he left resounded time and time again in his mind. He wondered how he and Aces got to this point.

CHAPTER NINETEEN

Aces and Spades

As Butcher sat at the table he tried to fit together the pieces. He continued to struggle with fitting together the fragmented pieces of his life. The missing pieces were that of lost loved ones. He without satisfaction tried to reason where he and Aces moved apart. He sat at the table in the quiet and lonely room and replied the visions in his head as if he was watching a movie.

Aces and Spades was the local bar that had the reputation for serving minors. He started going to the bar to play pool and drink beer at the age of 16. This was a crossroads in his life after Noah died and his family was becoming fractioned.

He would walk over behind the farm, over the ridge to the next road. The bar was a mile down the road. The parking lot was at one time stoned but in the summer mostly dirt.

There were no windows. A small box with a large sign out front displaying a hand of cards spelling out "Aces and Spades".

Peter had a rancorous argument with his mother for one reason or another and walked away. He walked until he reached the road behind his farm. This was the same road where the bar was located. He walked down the road and saw a lineup of motorcycles. The bikes were lined perfectly aside one another. The chrome shone bright in the summer sun. It Reflected the shadow of all the other bikes as they stood lined and proud. The bikes were beautiful he thought to himself. "I wonder who owns them?" As he opened the bar, the smoke-filled air from within whirled around and out the door as it met with the fresh air.

The door slammed shut behind him, shining a brief ray of light into the dark bar.

All insiders looked as the light interrupted their conversations like a rude intruder. Peter felt the strain of the stares as he entered the bar. Peter felt angry, scared yet curious. The onlookers glanced at the young man momentarily and then refocused on their business at hand.

Peter walked past the men playing pool. He noticed another group of men playing darts.

The bar was all but empty. He sat in the middle stool.

The bartender turned toward him looking directly into his young unsure eyes. It was palpable to the bartender that the boy a minor. Peter spoke loud and with false confidence, "Duquesne Draft and a shot." The bartender did not move nor react. He just looked at him.

Peter was not quite sure what he was waiting for but he did not look away. He did not repeat himself. He simply stared back. After a second the bartender turned and walked toward the drafts. He poured him a glass of beer and walked back. He slammed the glass down on the bar. "That will be $.50," he stated. Peter reached into his front pocket and pulled out a rumpled dollar bill. He set it on the bar. He did not want to hand it to the man directly. He was well premeditated in his actions. He had heard stories from the boys at school about how to bet served. He set the money down, picked up the beer and turned away.

He drank the beer as he worried internally about the bartender's next move. Desperately trying not to show his nerves he gulped the beer. He did not stop drinking it until the glass was half empty. He set the glass down on the bar and settled into the warm dizzy feeling that was enveloping his body. He looked around at the men in the bar. "So, these are the bikers," he thought to himself. "I wonder what they do to afford those kick ass bikes," He noticed the men playing darts. They were loud. They appeared to be drunk. All the men in the bar were dressed the same and looked basically the same. Not like his father or the other farmers on the street. He felt comfortable. They did not notice him and he felt as if he fit in. He watched and imbibed the atmosphere.

He turned back and finished his beer. He asked the bartender for another. The man walked back over without speaking to him. He picked up his glass and walked back over to the draft beer and poured a second glass. He walked back toward Peter and set it down on the bar in front of him. Peter noticed the single was still on the bar where he had left it.

He reached over and moved the bill toward the bartender. He still did not pick it up.

As Peter looked at the bartender he overhead the two men playing darts, as they moved toward the bar. They were arguing. He turned slightly and looked at them. They had been in an inebriated fueled argument. Over what, he could not comprehend. He turned to look at the older man who was shouting obscenities at the other.

"You're a fucking lying cunt Grygo!" He pushed the other man and he stumbled back toward Peter. He fell and Peter's beer spilled out of the glass and onto his shirt. He jumped up out of natural reaction.

"What the fuck is wrong you boy? I heard your momma calling you for dinner, run along home," the older man yelled out at Peter. Peter did not react although he was humiliated and angry. He was filled with rage and sick of men demeaning him. He thought of his father and his fear and repression. He was overcome with anger and rage. He looked around the bar and all other men stopped their actions and were focusing on him. They were focusing on the older man chastising him.

He pushed away from the bar and wiped the beer off of his shirt. The old man laughed. "That's it, go home to momma's tit!" He laughed. All of the other men laughed. The entire bar was laughing, at him.

Peter turned and walked calmly without speaking to the dartboard. The laughter did not stop. He did not hear it anymore. He had tuned it out. The reached out to the dartboard and pulled a dart from the foam board. The turned and held the dart down low at his side. He calmly walked back over to his barstool. He picked up his now half empty beer and drank it until the glass ran empty. He turned to leave. He walked past the first man who had bumped into him and walked past the older man. "Go home boy!" he said as he passed him. Peter quickly turned upon moving one foot past him. With a fist clenched with the dart, he plunged the dart into the man's cheek. The older man screamed in pain. The others did not comprehend what had just happened. The old men grabbed at his face that was squirting with blood. Peter stood in front of the man waiting for his reaction. He was ready to defend himself. The three men that were playing pool ran over, two grabbed Peter and the other braced the older man to ascertain what had happened.

As the scene became chaotic the bartender moved quickly from behind the bar to break up the men that were about to embark in a free for all brawl. "Enough!" the bartender screamed. When he did they seemed to immediately stop and listen to him.

"Grygo, Duke, Fritz go back to what you were doing. "Let the boy go."

He grabbed the men that were holding Peter ready to strike. They released their grip on him and the bartender grabbed him by the back of the shirt. "Come on," he pulled Peter by the shirt out the side door of the bar. He kicked the metal door open with the heel of his boot. Peter noticed the large tattoo on his forearm. 1%.

As the two men bounded out of the smoky dark bar, the sunlight hit Peter's eyes as he stumbled out of the bar after being thrown through the door by the bartender. The velocity of the throw forced Peter to his knees. "What the fuck are you doing? Are you stupid or just young, or both?" The bartender screamed at him. Peter did not have a chance to answer. He did not have a chance to get up. The bartender kicked him in the ribs and he fell to the ground. "You are in my fucking bar, under age, starting shit with my men? Who the fuck do you think you are?" Peter did not answer.

"Who the fuck do you think you are?" he asked again.

Peter regained his composure and stood up. "I am Peter Bauchmann, that's who the fuck I am." He yelled out. "I do not care who you are or who he is, I do not take shit from anyone. I didn't do anything to him. Fuck him!" He yelled back.

The bartender stood his ground looking at him, analyzing him. "I don't want any trouble. I am out of here." Peter turned and started to limp away. He took five to six steps and the bartender called out to him. "Stop." "Get back here." Peter was not up to fighting with the bartender. He seemed fair, strong and competent. He stopped and turned back. He did not know why he felt compelled to walk back to him. He respected the man's actions and control.

"What?" he asked.

"Where do you live?" He asked.

"Why do you want to call my parents? Don't bother they don't give a fuck anyway." He replied.

"That's not what I asked you." The bartender said calmly.

"I live over the ridge. I live on the Bauchmann farm." He reluctantly spoke up.

"Isn't that the farm where the young boy and horse where killed by the old man?" he asked.

"So you heard, what else is new?" he mumbled back. "Yeah, that's me."

"You got balls boy." The bartender extended his hand. "My name is Aces, I own this bar."

Peter reached out and shook his hand. He did not speak. "I respect what you did. It was cold but deserving." He said to Peter. "You are very collected for a young boy. I can use a person like you." he said.

"For what?" Peter asked. "I am the president of group of men. We have a business. All those bikes out there are ours." He explained. "Do you ride?" he asked Peter.

"I have but I cannot afford a bike," Peter replied.

He handed Peter his single. "Take your money. The drinks are on me. Come back tomorrow same time. We will talk more." Peter looked him in the eyes. The man was old and harsh yet he had warm eyes. He looked at him when he spoke. Peter was not used to that. His father was always busy doing other things when he spoke to him and never looked him in the eyes. His father never looked him in the eyes since the day Noah died. Peter looked at his wrist as he took the money from his hand. He was mesmerized by a tattoo of a hand of cards. He was sure the man was aware that he was staring at his tattoos. He put the money back into the front pocket of his jeans and looked away.

"Sure," he said. "I will be back tomorrow, same time." He turned and walked away.

Aces watched him walk away and turned to go back inside the bar to calm the men down. As the president of the SKALDS, his wishes would be respected. "That boy has potential," he said to himself as he walked back into the bar to calm the unruly men.

As Peter walked home he was still buzzing from the alcohol. He was still filled with adrenaline from the fight. He was feeling high from the compliments. He had not heard such adulation from anyone before. He felt respect for this man. He was strong. He complimented him. He saw something in Peter, his strength. These were feelings and emotions he no longer felt at home from his own father. He counted the minutes and hours until the next day when he would return to the Aces and Spades to meet with Aces. He later learned that Aces was the president of a large biker gang known as the Skalds. He led a local chapter and had significant power and influence. That is not what led him to him though. Aces showed an interest in him. When he spoke, he spoke with honesty and veracity. Peter admired his strength and the way he handled people. He demonstrated this that day.

As he sat recalling the day they met he could still feel the admiration and respect that they had for one another. He wondered if that had changed. If it had, when did it changed? He loved Aces and he knew through Aces tacit actions that he reciprocated the feelings. He felt the distance now and was longing for companionship. He knew he would not find it anytime soon. He walked over to the refrigerator and opened another beer and sat back down at the kitchen table, staring off into nothingness.

CHAPTER TWENTY

Christmas Morning

Rudi awoke to an envelope lying on Luke's empty pillow. He had left for work already. She was so tired and mentally exhausted from the trip to Houston that she did not hear him preparing for work that morning. She looked at the pillow, then at the card. She smiled assuming it would be a thoughtful sentiment from her assiduous husband. She grabbed the card off the pillow but paused before opening it. She smiled at the mere thought of not having to call the office, go online or stress over her juggling act with the farm and career. "Wow, this is it. I am unemployed. How great is this!" She said to herself in proud recognition of the facts. She removed herself from the warm, soft surroundings of her bed. She held the note and made her way down the stair to the kitchen.

As she entered the large shiny new kitchen she smelled the coffee that had been set on a timer for her. Luke did not drink coffee but would always turn it on as he left for it to fresh brew by the time she woke up. The aroma of the rich bold coffee filled the large kitchen space. She poured herself a cup and savored the moment of drinking it with no rushed agenda. She could actually sit, enjoy the coffee and read Luke's card.

She pulled out the chair to the marble table and sat the cup down. She carefully unfolded the back of the envelope as she was planning to add this to her scrapbook, the meticulous scrapbook that she had started when she and Luke first learned that their offer on the farm was accepted. The first page of the memory book was the memo taken by her assistant that stated, "Call Lois from Pennsylvania, good news, it's yours. (Whatever that means?) Sarah."

She opened the card to find a handwritten note.

"To a career well done and ended."

"To a new life and career now starting."

"Please meet me for dinner tonight to celebrate, at Vino's."

Love, Luke.

Vino's was a local Italian restaurant that had exceptionally good cuisine and a romantic atmosphere. She giggled out loud as she thought to herself, "He's so great. How exciting, a date." She sat and drank her coffee before ascending back up the stairs to change for the barn chores, her newly appointed position as stable hand was waiting.

Rudi spent the day mucking the stalls, grooming the horses and conditioning her tack. Tasks that she never thought she would have time for. She cleaned the house, drank a glass, or two, of wine and began to dress for her date. As she completed her preparation by misting herself with Luke's favorite scent the phone rang. It was Luke. She answered expecting him to say he was within minutes of the farm.

"Yes?" she answered.

"Hello sweetheart," Luke replied.

"Where are you?" Rudi asked.

"Unfortunately I am running late. I will be another hour at least." He sounded reluctant in his speech.

"No…" she whined out loud. "That totally sucks Luke." She disappointedly responded to his unsuccessful attempt to make the situation acceptable.

"I will hurry and meet you in one hour. I promise. In the meantime, I cannot find my new sunglasses." He commented, preparing himself for an incensed response from his wife.

"The very expensive ones that I just bought for you? Those sunglasses?" she annoying replied.

"Yes Rudi, those ones. Can you please go into the upper barn and see if I left them on the ledge?" he begged of her. "Okay, you are taking the piss right? I am dressed in high heels to go out and you want me to go into the barn to look for your very expensive, newly purchased as a gift, sunglasses that may, or may not be in the dirty dusty barn? And did I add a very thoughtful and expensive gift from your otherwise very patient wife?" she spoke to him with sarcasm. "

Yes, you pretty much have it down, where is the grey area?" He could not contain laughter as he uttered the words. "Put on your muck boots, the horses won't tell, go to the barn and see if they are there. Call me back because if they are not I have to search my office again for them."

"Fine." She was finished with the sentence. She hung up on him in frustration. She marched down the steps stopping only to gather a quick necessity, a glass of white wine from the refrigerator. She poured herself a glass as she condemned him, aloud. She made her way into the mudroom and removed her black sling back shoes. She slipped her feet into her dirty muck boots that were scented not with Luke's favorite perfume—but horse manure.

She mumbled as she made her way to the barn with the cordless phone in one hand and the glass of white wine in the other. She reached the upper barn door. Opening the large sliding doors required her placing the wine and phone on the ground. She uttered one additional profanity aimed at Luke before using strength and agility to disjoint her strapless dress. "I am going to fucking kill you Luke Hudson."

As the door sluggishly opened along the rusted track she reached in to turn on the lights.

As the light illuminated the barn, hanging strings of fairy lights cascading down from the 40-foot wood rafters drifted to the ground where they were secured to the floor. She looked at the lights in disbelief and confusion. Her eyes followed the light that flowed to the center of the barn then to the floor. There in the center of the room was a small round table with a crisp white linen tablecloth. A single orchid stood in a vase in the center of the perfectly set table. She glanced to her right then to the left where Luke was stood in the corner with the look of an ornery schoolboy. He laughed out loud as she looked at him with shock and disbelief.

He walked toward her and held out his hand. "To Rudi's first day as the curator of Brown Hill Farm." She was so dazed that she overlooked the title that he had placed on the farm. He grabbed her and pulled her into his arms.

"You are so crazy, screwing with my head like that." She yelled at him. "This is so awesome. I cannot believe you did this! When?" she asked of him.

"I have been planning this for months." He proudly announced.

"Where did you call me from just minutes ago?" she questioned him trying to make sense of the plot. "I called you from the barn from my cell phone. I was in the barn all along." He informed her.

There she stood, in a strapless black dress and muck boots. She looked down at her feet and started to laugh. Luke broke away from the embrace to pour her a glass of champagne from the ice bucket that housed two opened bottles. He handed her the glass and said, "A toast." She laughed as she took the glass from his hand.

"To my beautiful wife, standing in her new place of employment in an $800 designer dress and muck boots, looking as beautiful as ever." He clinched his glass against hers. She allowed a tear to fall from her eyes as she smiled and casually brushed it away.

"This is so unbelievable and beautiful. I love you more than words can describe." She replied quietly.

Luke ushered Rudi over to the table. He pulled out her chair. "So what is on the menu?" she asked. She could not understand how he could pull off serving hot food.

"Ah, you just wait my dear." He replied as he pulled out his cell phone. The keypad sounded out eleven beeps as he placed the phone to his ear.

"We are ready."

Rudi looked on smiling and shaking her head in disbelief. She thought to herself, "No woman deserves all of this, but I am glad it's me."

Within minutes she heard a car approach from the sound of the rumbling stones on the driveway. A waiter and two men in chef's jackets began hastily setting up a table, burners, chafing dishes and semi-prepared food.

"I had the chef at Vino's prepare us a meal for takeout. I hope you don't mind." He smiled as he asked her.

"No, I certainly do not."

Hors d'oeuvres, salad, veal and dessert were prepared for the two of them in the intimate, romantic setting of the 120-year-old barn. The two laughed, kissed and embraced not only each other but the magical atmosphere that the hayloft and barn rafters offered. "This part of the barn is beautiful." Rudi commented. She went on to add, "I do not know if I would have ever seen it in such a romantic light. It is amazing."

Luke agreed but his mind was preoccupied with his next surprise.

He stood up from the table and said to Rudi, "One moment. I have to get something." She looked at him wide eyed not expecting what he could possibly do to top his latest.

Luke walked over to the wall that separated their space by the hayloft. He reached around and pulled out a large flat item. It was wrapped in brown recycled paper. He walked over to Rudi and handed the large present to her. "Oh, as if the dinner, champagne and personal waiter service wasn't enough." She acerbically replied.

"This is a small gift so that you always remember this evening. Rudi, you quit your career to come to this unknown town and revive this farm. You have put your heart and soul into that house. You have singlehandedly saved two horses that live downstairs." He paused and smiled placing his hand to his ear. "We can hear them eating at this very moment. Not many, wait, scratch that, I do not know of any one person that would make such a drastic change to their seemingly perfect life to undertake this project. I cannot take much credit. You have done all the work. I admire you for jumping off and following your heart."

His speech was met with appreciation. Rudi could not believe that Luke was so in tune with her actions, thoughts and desires. He truly understood the meaning of the move, the hardship, the energy and strength it took and was still consuming, to fulfill this dream.

She reached out and took the present. She ripped open the paper and unveiled a large black and white framed picture in a beautiful hand carved frame with silver leafing. She looked at the picture for several seconds attempting to decipher it before commenting.

The photo was of a family. A woman, man, boy, girl and younger boy. They were stood in front of a white picket three-railed fence. A small horse grazed in the background. The family had on winter coats but was dressed in holiday apparel.

"Who is this?" she asked.

"It is a photo of the family that lived her for two generations. The grandfather of the man you see built the farm. This is his family. We purchased the farm from the daughter you see there." He had his facts prepared and was pointing to the figures as he explained the history.

"These are the Bauchmann's. The husband was named Joe and the wife's name was Melinda. They had three children here. I contacted the woman who sold the property. She gave me this photograph and I had it enlarged and framed. I thought it would be inspirational and meaningful to you. Oh, I almost forgot, they called the farm Brown Hill Farm."

Rudi did not comment but recalled his earlier words to that effect. Now she understood what he had meant.

Rudi sat silent and did not comment immediately. She stared at the strangers. She tried to imagine their lives. Many times as she cleaned the barn or the attic she would come across an item that eluded to the prior history but she never had anything solid.

"I can't believe you found this, or dug this up. This means so much to me Luke." She placed the picture against the table so it would not fall and stood to embrace him. She held him close for minutes until he pulled away.

"There is more." He said.

"Bonnie Bauchmann, the woman in the photo, gave me her number. It is on the of the card. You can call her when you have time to do more research on the farm and history. Apparently there was some blight, crisis and all that torrid stuff that makes these old homes exciting." As he spoke Rudi turned the picture over and there was a card placed on the back with her name and contact information.

"Luke, this is the most thoughtful, meaningful gift I have ever received in my life. I do not know what to say. I only hope I make you as happy during your lifetime as you made me." She said.

She did not know how to reply, repay or move forward. Rudi did not possess the thoughtful attention to detail traits that Luke had. She loved Luke but did not rise to his level of expression. She had always known that one person in a relationship loves deeper than the other. The two are never equal. In this relationship it was evident to both of them that it was Luke. Rudi felt guilty for a moment but did not want to alter the mood that he so arduously set.

"I love you. I do not deserve you." She said before she kissed him. "This will be one on the most special moments of my life." She said aloud.

The two embraced and felt a connection that transcended their existing relationship while embracing in the barn. They made love that night, in the hayloft. It felt right, as if they were not the first.

CHAPTER TWENTY-ONE

The Center Piece Of The Puzzle

Rudi's thoughts often drifted to the experience at the airport both in Houston and in Pittsburgh. Days had passed and she had not heard from the FBI. She had assumed that her continued participation was not necessary. That did not disappoint her.

She was back home and busy with the details of completing the barn, pastures and home.

It was a beautiful spring morning. She had finished the chores of the barn and was sitting at the table drinking a cup of coffee while planning her day. As she made a note of days chores the telephone rang. She had already placed it on the table preparing for the calls she had to make.

She picked up the phone and called the first name on her list. The painter was the first on the list.

Rudi hung up the telephone after leaving yet another voicemail. She heard the tone indicating that a call had come in while she was leaving the third message for the painter.

She put in the numbers to her voicemail system. She repeated the automated message indicating a call, "One call?" She listened to the message. As she did, she sat in disbelief feeling that she had somehow brought the call to fruition.

"Ms. Hudson, my name is Tom Carderos. I work for the Federal Bureau of Investigations in Houston Texas. Please call me at your earliest convenience. It is regarding your interview with Federal Air Marshal Mark Stinton. I have some additional questions for you. I can be reached at 713-555-9950."

She replayed the message. When she had heard the voicemail a third time she saved it. She sat the phone on the table and stared straight ahead. She was worried. She was now back at home and the reality of the situation was more serious than she thought. "What can happen to me, Luke, the horses if this man is a wanted person?" she asked herself. "He lives somewhere around here?" She spoke to herself. She was convinced that the situation was no longer dismissed as crazy excitement. She felt concerned for her welfare and all associated with her.

She did not return the call. She picked up the phone to call Luke. "Luke Hudson," she heard on the other line. Just the mere announcement and sound of his voice was soothing and reassuring.

"Luke, it's me."

"Hey, what's up?" he asked without any concern. Rudi often called Luke during the day.

"An FBI agent called me. Two fucking minutes ago." She frantically informed him.

"Well, didn't they say that they would call?" he asked her calmly in an attempt to appear paregoric.

"That was weeks ago."

"Six days Rudi, not weeks," he corrected her.

"This is not good. What if they want me to testify and this guy, this biker wacko comes after us." She rambled on.

"Rudi, calm down."

"Don't tell me to calm down." She replied.

Rudi only said that when she was angry or very upset. Normally when Luke told her to calm down she would.

"Did you call him?" he asked.

"No," she replied.

"Why not?" he questioned her.

"I do not want to deal with it," She stated.

"If you do not deal with it, it will not go away. Why don't you call them to see if it they just want to clarify something? Maybe this is all for nothing." He tried to calm her down.

He was concerned. He did not want her or them to get involved with a member of a notorious biker gang. A biker gang member who was wanted by the FBI could not be a good scenario.

"I can't call yet. Is that bad?" she wanted his approval to dismiss the call.

"I cannot tell you to ignore them Rudi. If you want to wait a day or two I am sure the world will not end. Can you please wait until I am with you and we will call them together?"

"Okay. Gotta Go. Love you. Bye." She hung up.

Luke laughed out loud. "She calls me and then dumps me," he said to himself. He knew that Rudi was nervous and scared. That concerned him. He did not return to work immediately. He sat and thought. He thought about her, the situation and attempted to work out a dialog that she could use when returning the FBI's call.

He picked up the phone and called her back. She answered. "Rudi, don't worry. I have a list of questions and a scripted answer that you can use when we call the fed's back. I will not let anything happen to you or us," he reassured her.

"Thanks. I know I am wigged out. I am sorry for dumping you like that. I just didn't know if I was doing the right thing by not calling them back. Like, can they arrest me or anything?" she asked.

"No. I will call James King though." James King was an attorney that Luke's company used. He was personal friends with him. "I will pass this by him and see what he says. I do not want you to be freaked out though. Do you hear me?"

"Yes," she replied.

"I love you Rudi," he told her.

"Love you too," She said and hung up. She picked the phone back up and dialed another number. The phone was ringing.

***

Peter's phone rang. He looked at the caller ID and noted that it was Dempsey. He answered, "Yeah?"

"Be there in five," said Dempsey. Before Peter was aware of the time that had passed the throttle of Dempsey's bike sounded out his arrival. He stood up and walked towards the door. He was not looking forward to setting out the plans for yet another hit with Dempsey. Not after the last one went so tits up as he put it in his mind's eye.

He opened the door before Dempsey knocked or entered. That tactile move gave him the smallest feeling of power. Dempsey walked in. Butcher looked out into the woods as he always did just to make sure there was nothing out of the ordinary or anyone following Dempsey. The cabin was far set into the woods. Even if he one was to follow him on the main roads, once in the woods the narrow winding paths that accommodated the motorcycles lent themselves to camouflage. Cars had difficulty navigating the roads that lead to the cabin. That did not stop Butcher from being paranoid.

Dempsey pulled out the chair and sat at the table. He slammed his hand down on the wood table, "Let's go around again Butcher because you fucked this up the last time." As he removed his hand a bag of white powder was left behind.

"Cut me a line and let's sort out the details." He ordered Butcher. Butcher knew the protocol. The one that cut the lines was the servant. He was not in the position to argue with Dempsey but he was not in the normal "take it up the ass" mood. He laughed and said, "Is this your shit or Aces shit?" If it's yours, I have my own." This was a clear insult to the second man. It was a small jab to let Dempsey know that he was aware and that he should not lose sight that Aces is still on top.

"Fuck you, do your own then. The more for me." He pulled a gas credit card out of his wallet and cut his own line. He rolled up a five dollar bill and snorted the one line.

"So, how do you feel about going home?" He said after he held his nostrils shut and sucked in all the surrounding air from his immediate air space.

"What are you talking about?" replied Butcher.

"Your home, the mark's address. Didn't Aces give you the address?" Dempsey was too busy cutting his second line to bother looking at Butcher's confused face.

"Yeah, the address is Canterbury or Canterbury Lane. So what?" He replied with confidence refusing to allow Dempsey to dismantle his strength.

Dempsey did not answer. He wanted to snort the second line. He did. Paused then looked up at Butcher. It dawned on him that he did not know that Canterbury Lane was RR 709.

"You stupid mother fucker. 909 Canterbury Lane was RR 709. Ring any bells you stupid cunt?" He was laughing as he mocked Butcher.

Butcher grabbed him by the jacket and pulled him off of his seat. Butcher was larger and heavier than Dempsey. Pound for pound Butcher was the stronger of the two men. He never exalted his advantage out of respect for Aces. This was different. He was being taunted and his childhood was not fair game.

Dempsey reacted as expected. He laughed. "What are you going to do Butcher? Take me out back and chop me up? Yeah, the mark lives at your old house. They changed the rural routes last year. You are going to have to get your head around this. You are the man who has to finish this business. If you fuck this one up, not even Aces can save your sorry ass Butcher."

Butcher let go of the tight grasp on the collar of his jacket. He turned and stared at the floor. "Fuck this, I am not going back there." He spoke to himself. He would not allow Dempsey to hear him.

The room was silent. Butcher paced the floor like a wolf. circling the same area while pondering, questioning and attempting to comprehend and make sense of the situation.

"Look Butcher, it is what it is. Get your shit together. We have to lay out this plan. Do your deal and then cry about it later." Dempsey sensed that he had to pull Butcher back together. He had pushed the man far enough. It was time to reel him back in.

He dumped the powder on the table. "Here, sit down, snort this line and let's get through this." He sifted through the coke with the gas card. He cut Butcher a huge line with the hopes of luring him back to the table. Butcher did not turn. He stood firm.

He was calculating the percentage of chance that would permit this. "What would be the reason for this?" he asked himself. "Okay, big fucking deal. I know someone bought the farm. So it was the lady from the airport in Houston." He was frantically attempting to convince himself that the odds and fate of this blow from Dempsey was not fatal.

He turned. Walked over to the refrigerator and grabbed a beer. He twisted the cap and drank it. He drank the entire bottle before sitting back down. When the bottle was empty he threw it into the old porcelain sink. The sound of the thick glass rattling against the porcelain echoed his feelings of anger. He opened the refrigerator and grabbed another beer. He twisted off the top and sat down. The pulled his hair back off of his face with his left hand and used his right hand to snort the line with Dempsey's rolled up bill.

"You okay man?" Dempsey asked.

"Fine, what's the plan?" He replied without emotion. "Let's do this so I can get the fuck out of this hell hole. I am sick of being holed up here. The sooner I do this, the sooner I can move on."

Dempsey was lifted by his positive comment. There were moments that he felt the plan would have to change and Aces would have to find another man for this job. The truth to the matter was that Butcher was the best hit man he had ever worked with. The best the gang used. He was professional, strong, emotionless and cold. He performed hits that echoed throughout the gang and other social groups in similar circles.

"I have been watching the girl," Commented Dempsey with a large grin on his face. "That fucking horse of hers almost did this job for you." He laughed as he recalled Rudi falling from the horse as he watched from the woods. "I fucking hate horses and horses hate me." Dempsey veered off course from the current subject. "You know, even as kid I hated them and they hated me. I think they sense it. You know, I think that big fucking dumb animal knew I was in the woods. He reared up and threw her right in front of me." He repeated the falling incident.

"They mustn't be that fucking stupid then, are they Dempsey?" replied Butcher as he sneered at him. He felt obligated to defend horses primarily with Coffee in the back of his mind.

"If the animal sensed you, and sensed danger, it has more intelligence than most of these stupid fucks that I whack, they never see it coming." He went on to venerate the honor of the animal and put down the likes of humans, mainly Dempsey.

"If you say so Butcher," he dismissingly replied. "Like I said, I've watched the lady and her old man for awhile. There are no kids. She goes into the barn at night. The husband is a suit. He's home every night. You will have to get in quick and get out. The barn as you know has a back exit into the woods."

Dempsey had the plan well thought out. This was his job though as he was more than an interested party. He had as much chance of going down as Butcher if this woman was left to serve as a witness.

Butcher felt calmer with the effects of the alcohol and coke. He did not speak. He listened to Dempsey. He was determined to finish this and move on.

"Take the bike to the dumpster at 70 Plaza. I will call you after she gets into the barn. If you take back road you will get to the farm in 5-10 minutes. She's in there dicking around for 45 sometimes an hour." He was methodical.

"Didn't you have horses? What was the name of the horse that your Dad chopped up?" He was high and overly aggressive. Dempsey's personality grew larger and more obnoxious with the more coke he snorted. He had done two large lines in such a short period of time this night; his comments were sharp and bitter.

"What if the husband comes out?" asked Butcher. He was not going to gratify Dempsey's questions. "Coffee," he said to himself. "The horses name was Coffee."

"What does Aces want to do if the husband comes out?" He asked again.

Butcher was a true professional who thought of all possible situations and had a plan so that situations did not dictate the fate of the mission.

"If the husband comes out do him also. Once I call you go to the gas access road just off Smithton Road. Pull off and take the access road. The truck will be there. The tools will be in the back. Leave your bike there. Walk to the barn. One to the head. Take the gun and body back to the truck. I will meet you there. We will bury the evidence back in the woods behind the Shuster farm."

Dempsey was not going to take any more chances with Butcher being witnessed. He devised a plan where no one would be able to literally place Butcher in the vehicle where the body would be transferred to and from.

"Once you pop her one in the brain, bring her body back to the truck. Tarp her. I will meet you at the truck and we will throw her in the back and take her back to the old Miller property."

"Are we going to drive the truck there on the access road?" asked Butcher.

"Yeah. Once you get off of the main roads you will not get back on until she is done and buried." He replied.

"Yeah but have you checked it out lately? It might be overgrown. I don't want to scratch up the truck dumping her. I sure as hell don't want it to look like the trucks been driving through the woods." He questioned how solid Dempsey's plan was.

Dempsey grew up within close proximately of Butcher. The farms all sold gas rights to the local natural gas company. This company bought land and had access roads that lead form miles behind all the farms on the ridge. The roads were large enough for pickup trucks to travel on. Few people were aware of all the gas roads and even fewer used the land for personal use. The gas company checked wells, stayed to business and did not deviate from the main roads forged by the company that lead to their wells. The body would not be found if buried deep enough to escape coyote or other meat eating predators.

"I've been there. It's fine. Once you get her back to the truck we need to remove her head and hands. This cunt is now a Federal witness. If those pigs find her body she can't be identified. You're a specialist at dismemberment aren't you? Oh no that was your old man." He mocked Peter again.

"Sever her head and hands. We will bag and take them. Aces wants it. Seems he has lost some faith in you." He looked at Butcher with deep anger for tarnishing his reputation with the last bit of sloppy work.

"Once she's in the ground I take the truck to Rowdy's and he'll take it from there."

Rowdy was a brother who owned a body shop. He provided the vehicles and disposed of them for the gang.

"You leave the same way you came but push your bike over the hill and exit from the Miller access road instead of the Smithton access road. Don't start your bike up until you have pushed it 10-15 feet onto the road."

Butcher's mind was memorizing the plan and assuring the accuracy and legitimacy of the details. "Cut me another line," Butcher said. He was already feeling the tight grip of the past squeezing his chest. His breath felt short and his pulse rapid.

"Butcher," Dempsey stopped his thoughts from wandering too far as he could see his mind racing through the movement of his dilated pupils. As he spoke he cut two lines from the bag of coke. "If you fuck this up, you will go down. You will also take me down. And if that happens I will make sure you do not live five minutes in jail. You'll die with a knife in your chest as you take it up the ass." Dempsey was not joking with Butcher and he was fully aware of the sentiment.

He did not wait for Butcher to snort the line. He snorted one and tossed the bill at him.

"Aces will not tolerate another fuck up or for, YOU, to fuck up again."

"We are brothers out of our loyal pledge to the gang but we are not friends." He reminded Peter.

"No fuck Dempsey," was Peter's only response as he was more interested in snorting the line on the table than he was in receiving a chastising smack on the wrist from Dempsey.

Butcher looked at him coldly. He looked down at the line and snorted it. He looked up rubbing the powder from his nostrils and spoke as he rubbed his nose.

"I have the plan Dempsey now you can leave. I do not need a slumber party."

Butcher felt that he had held it together as long as he could. He wanted Dempsey to leave so he could be alone with his emotions and insecurities.

"I'm outta here. As long as you know the plan and don't fuck up." He got up and walked out. He did not speak to Butcher as he walked out.

Butcher heard the sound of his bike roar to a start. He waited until he heard the bike's exhaust faded into the distance.

He walked over to the bed and lay down. He turned to the wall. He began to cry. He did not sob. He cried, for himself. Maybe it was for Coffee and Noah, he did not know nor care. He did know however that he could not find a way out of this. He had to finish this. He knew he was strong enough to handle the job. He was bitter as to the hidden meaning as to why he had to handle the job.

Peter cried himself to sleep as he done when he was fourteen. Those countless long nights after Noah died. With mental anguish, he recalled the countless nights he lay awake in his bed listening to the descent of his parent's marriage and subsequently the fractioning of his family. His life changed that night and from then on he spent many nights laying in his bed sobbing and longing for the past and devoted much of his energy towards feeling anger and hatred. "The final piece of the puzzle is in the middle." He whispered Aces sentiment.

CHAPTER TWENTY-TWO

Presence Of Danger

Rudi realized that her call did not go through. After three rings she got a busy tone. She looked at the phone and noticed that she had lost reception. She turned off the phone concluding that the time was not right. "I'll go riding then call Luke when I get back to the barn." She thought. Her mood was not relaxed as she shut off her phone, laid it upon the ledge of the tack room and walked into Java's stall. Since her last day of work, Rudi felt disjointed. She was struggling with the transition from full time employment to nothing, as she often thought of it. Rudi was used to a hectic and busy schedule that demanded her time and attention. She was feeling a loss of significance. She thought or assumed that when she resigned employment she would feel liberated. She did not, at least not yet.

Once in Java's stall she grabbed his reins. She had put his halter on him over 40 minutes earlier. Java was also short on patience. He had been in a bit, saddle and head reins for too long now.

Rudi walked into the stall and grabbed his reins without speaking to him. She turned and walked Java out of the stall toward the gate that led to the woods. She wore jeans and chaps this day. She did not have the time or effort to put on the proper English riding apparel. She pulled the jeans down beneath the leather chaps and mounted Java. He sensed her anticipation and moved forward. She fell out of the stirrup and stumbled to the ground. "Fuck Java, stand still, I am in no mood." She chastised him. His large brown eyes looked over at her with bewilderment. He was not accustomed to this kind of treatment from her.

Once upon his back she kicked him on. He lunged forward up the path to the woods. There was a disconnection between them. Normally when she rode Billy or Java the bond between the two was communicated. This ride was disjointed and she did not relax to sense Java's mood. She wanted to exercise him and return to the house to finish chores, call Luke and organize the next day.

Java reached the top of the short hill at the clearing and stopped. He reared up and Rudi lost her balance being she was not in tune to his movement. As Java reared up, Rudi's equilibrium became unstable. She fell backwards out of the saddle. Her left leg caught in the stirrup and she twisted while on the ground to free her leg. Once Java realized that his mistress had fallen he did not move or attempt to flee. He was preoccupied with the sound. He sensed a presence. Rudi did not have a clue what rattled Java. She lay on the ground for seconds before standing. She attempted to grab his reins so he would not run away. Once she became aware that he was not in flight, she let go of the reins and tended to her immediate pain. She stood up.

"Java, that was out of control. What are you doing?" She walked over to him and yelled in his face. Her eyes were inches from his. She did not see the reflection in his eyes. His large eyes reflected the shadow of a strange figure in the brush. The figure was that of a man. Rudi grabbed the reins and questioned his actions. "What are you doing?" she continued with the inquisition. Java stood still staring at the stranger off to the left side of her tirade. Java was impervious to her scolding, he was fixated on the impending danger.

Rudi brushed off her jeans and ran her fingers through her hair attempting to regain composure. She tried to mount him on the spot and he did not allow her. He walked forward disconnecting her foot from the stirrup.

"Java!" She jerked his reins back. "Please stop!" she snapped at him. Java moved forward attempting to pass through the area he considered to be of a threat to him and her.

She allowed him to walk on for ten feet or so. She stopped and thought she heard movement. She turned her head toward the sound. "Maybe it was a deer. It was heavy. Not a turkey or bird," she thought to herself. She stopped silent. She heard another rustling of the branches that cluttered the forest ground. She was confident that it was a human and not an animal. Uncomfortable and insecure with her surroundings, she quickly placed her foot in the stirrup, as Java moved forward she quickly threw her leg over his back. He began to run, quickly driven by fear. Rudi was not reacting on fear. She grabbed his reins and they ran quickly through the woods until they reached a clearing some 100 yards away. Rudi did not look back until the two of them reached the open field. She slowed Java down then to a stop. She dismounted him and calmed herself down. She tried to make reason of the last five minutes.

She walked over to Java and spoke to him. "What did you see?" she asked him. "I should have paid attention to you." She said to herself as if Java would comprehend her comment. "Fuck me, that was bad." She continued. Java was spooked and so was she. She knew that there was a stranger in the woods. A presence that was not innocent. She could not place her finger on it, she just sensed it.

After a few minutes passed and once she sensed that they both had calmed down she once again mounted Java. They walked for a mile or so through the flat field. She turned him around and they both made pace for the barn. Once upon the spot where Java sensed the intruder she slowed him down and then to a stop. He did not resist her. This trip back she was in tune to his muscular reactions. She admitted to herself that she was negligent in reading his reactions earlier. She walked him on toward the spot where she thought the stranger stood. She attempted to inspect the ground for signs of his presence.

As she walked around the circumference of the area she noticed that the grass had been stamped down. She knelt down to pick up a turquoise green object. It was the butt of filtered cigarette. She picked up the object and moved it upwards to her nose. She smelled the end to see if it was fresh. It was. She could smell the ashy smell of a recently stomped out cigarette. She placed the butt in the pocket of her jeans. She looked around with an uncomfortable feeling. She did not know if he had fled or if he was still watching. "Why was he here?" she commented to herself.

She was aware that hunters scoped out the area but this was different. She sensed an uncomfortable aura in the air. She looked over at Java who was twitching. His ears perked. His nostrils were flared and ready for flight. She quickly walked back to him, soothed him by patting his forehead and mounted him. Once back in the barn she removed his saddle, reins and moved swiftly to exit the barn toward the house.

When she settled inside the house she attempted to call Luke again. This time he answered. "Hello?" he said.

"Wow, I am glad you answered," she replied.

"Why?" he asked of her.

"I had a freaky ride. I cannot place my finger on it but it was weird. I think someone was scoping out the barn or the woods." She said as awkward as it sounded.

"Well, did you see anyone?" Luke asked.

"Not really. I saw a reflection in Java's eye. He freaked out and we ran. When we returned to the spot I found a smoldering cigarette butt." She explained. "There definitely was someone there." She went on to convince him.

"I am on my way home. Stay in the house until I get there. I will walk out back with you. Those hunters are nuts. I am sure it was just a redneck spotting for the best deer spot." He tried to calm his wife.

"You are probably right, but it still freaked me and Java out. I fucking hate that these idiots sit on our property. It is crazy that we moved from such a suburban area where we had no privacy to an area where people can hide in our backyard. It's nuts."

"Okay, have a glass of wine. I will see you in 50 minutes. Are you okay?" Luke asked.

"Yes, I am fine." She replied. "I promise I will be adequately inebriated by the time you arrive home." She jokingly commented.

"Love you." Luke replied before disconnecting the call.

"Love you too." Replied Rudi as she hung up.

CHAPTER TWENTY-THREE

All Paths Lead Back Home

The next few days came and went. Peter waited for Dempsey's call. He was never at rest. Every second of every minute kept hectic pace with his pulse. He could not rest knowing at any minute he would be called to return to the source of his pain to perform yet another killing.

The stress and reality of the situation plagued his mind and clouded the reality of his life.

First the first time since his adolescence he longed to go back and relive the years he lost. He wanted to regain the adolescent years where he was obsessed with anger. Peter would stare at his father with accusing stares hoping to stir up feelings of guilt. That effort was futile. Peter tried assiduously to where lost from this point forth. He shook his head in disbelief at all the lost time he spent as a misguided teenager expressing unexplainable outbursts of aggression. He recognized that he has become an even angrier disturbed adult. He blamed loosing the adoration that he once felt for his mother. His instincts always told him that she knew more than she professed to know. He never asked her nor spoke of that night with her. He formed a protective shield over himself as a reaction to his parent's cold detachment and abandonment from him and his sister.

As he lay watching the small television that sat in the far corner the cabin, he became disturbed with the thought how long he had been isolated at the shack. It was not much different that a jail cell to him. He was left there, no contact with others and communication only from few select people. Although he could literally come and go as he pleased he had to stay out of sight. That prevented him from having the freedom of coming and going as he liked.

He thought of the disappointment that began to mount after he became the number one hit man for the Skalds. He did not esteem to become the man he did within the gang. He wanted a family. He wanted a group of people that cared for him, would fight for him, laugh with him and share life with him. He did not think he would spend so much of his time alone, away from his brothers.

His cell phone rang out announcing the one person who would be summoning him at this time. He did not answer it. He looked at the caller ID and identified the caller with the deed. It was time.

"This is my last deed for awhile, business is business," he told himself as he gathered his necessary objects. Before he walked out the door he looked around the cabin with hope that things would begin to change after this one. He placed his feet on the ground and took in a deep breath. He did not visually imagine the appearance of the farm. He tried to disassociate with the reality that he would be returning to the place where he grew up. Where Noah died. Where he saw his father murder his younger brother. "It's just another place, another hit," He uttered the words aloud. He had 30 minutes to arrive at the first contact spot. He could not be late. He could not be diverted.

He walked over to the coffee can and removed the parcel of coke and another parcel of pills. Tonight he would need both. The air was cool but spring scents filled the air and evoked memories of his childhood. The woods smelled of honeysuckle.

The crickets broke the silence of the night. As he drove away from the cabin the breeze shook the petals of the wild cherry blossoms off of their bloom. They swirled in the air and climbed downward towards the ground. He looked up and at that moment thought it looked like snow just as he did when he was young. He drove off into the dark away from the cabin toward what he thought was a turning point toward a better life. He had convinced himself that his time would be the last. At least for a while.

He arrived at the first waiting spot. It was void of activity. The rain had ceased and a slight fog loomed over the lower part of the atmosphere making the abandon shopping mall even more quite and strange. Strip malls have an unnerving, eerie presence after daylight leaves. They were meant for people and activity. At night they transform into strange quiet structures where visitors are no longer welcome.

There Butcher would wait, for hours maybe. He would wait for Dempsey to call and tell him that it was time. As Butcher waited, he sensed the presence of his father. His thoughts drifted to the cold, austere figure. Most described Joe as having a lack of presence but to Peter he had a very distinguishable presence. It was one of intimidation and judgment that struck fear deep into his heart. Butcher was always fragile, quiet and inept around his father. The least he said, the safer he felt. The unnatural quietness of the back of the strip mall reminded him of how the atmosphere was when he was in the presence of his father.

There he sat on his motorcycle with his feet straddled, muscles tense and feet firmly pressed onto the asphalt. The black asphalt was wet glistening and reflecting the white hue of the street lights overhead. The shadows of the empty buildings that stood behind him loomed over his own shadow portraying him as dark and disfigured.

As he stood and waited, dragging from his cigarette, he looked at the large commercial dumpster as it overflowed with debris. The ground was littered with soggy cigarette packs and plastic bottle caps that had been dismembered from the bottle. The light in front of the dumpster shown down through the transparent plastic soda bottles glistening off the brown liquid left inside.

Butcher thought of the trash that surrounded him. Not the debris that spewed from the dumpster or the bottles that were discarded without attention to their proper disposal place but of the people that he destroyed. They were shameless worthless human forms of trash that littered his life and that of those around him. He stood in dark wet symbolism that was the reality of his life. He would spend the next hour discarding of a woman just as perfunctory as the brown synthetic butts of cigarette filters that were flung to the ground beside him.

The damp, quiet eerie surroundings were combining with the drugs in his system and mercurially altering his sedate mood. His phone sounded jolting him from his deep destructive thoughts.

He answered the phone this time.

"Yep?"

Butcher answered with a statement of affirmation instead of question.

"Go pick up the pizza, it's ready, now."

Dempsey spoke the one sentence before the call disconnected.

Butcher reached into the pocket of his leather jacket and felt around for a pill. He pulled out a white pill and swallowed it. He reached back into his pocket for another object, his bullet. This was a small object that was filled with cocaine. When tapped upside down, the powder would fill a chamber and the drug could be snorted directly from the vile without removing it.

Butcher had always made it a rule not to get overly drunk, high or sedated before doing a hit. This job was different. He was fully aware that he could not perform his duties this time unless he felt nothing, or if he could subdue the pain he was feeling inside maybe he would not care. He snorted the bullet with each nostril. He continued to sit on his bike, in the dark, until the drugs started to perform their job so that he could perform his.

When Butcher arrived at the second spot he could see the pickup truck just ahead. As he got closer he noticed Dempsey was standing against the truck. Peter drove up to the vehicle and turned off his bike. He got off and walked over to where Dempsey was leaning.

"What are you doing here?" he asked. Dempsey had deviated from the plans. He was not supposed to meet him until after the hit. He was questioning why Dempsey was there. He thought with a hint of rare optimism, "Maybe the hit is off."

As Butcher walked over to Dempsey he motioned with his head and shoulders, "What?"

"She's alone. The old man must be out of town. He has not been there for two days. I'll wait here until you call to bring her back. Grab the backpack from the back of the truck."

Dempsey was confident and pleased with the news that the woman's husband was out of town, removing the threat of complication.

Butcher walked around to the side of the truck and grabbed the backpack. He opened the black nylon nondescript bag and reached for gun. It was his usual modus operandi. A .38 caliber double automatic Colt.

"Do you have your brain together?" asked Dempsey. Butcher dropped the magazine from the gun. As it dropped into his palm he looked at the rounds and shoved it back into the gun with his palm in a defiant move.

"Fuck you Dempsey. I didn't ask you if you pissed yourself in the woods spying on the mark." He stuffed the gun into the front of his pants and walked toward the path. The path to the barn. The same path he took as a child. The same path he ran on with Noah. They would run home when they saw the sun falling behind the trees. The rain started to fall as he got further into the woods. He looked up. It made him think his father was spitting on his face. He started to run. "Fuck you!" he screamed out into the dark cold sky. As he ran on the path, the holes and divots filled with rain. His boots slammed into the puddles of water unsettling the small pools that lay on the path. The rain fell onto this face and dripped down his cheek. The rain felt like tears falling nonstop without end down his face.

"I have to be about four minutes from the barn," he said to himself in a moment of panic. He continued to run. The branches from the brambles slapped at his face and grabbed at his legs countering his movement forward. He pushed his hands in front of his face to protect himself from the attacking branches. Through the trees at the end of the path he saw the roof of the barn. The large cold structure.

He began to combine the rain dripping off his cheeks, nose and chin with tears. He could not contain the abundant emotional torment that afflicted his thoughts. Each step took him closer to his childhood. He felt pulled. Pulled toward the barn. He was running toward something but felt as if he was not orchestrating his movements. Before he could analyze his feelings and how he should deal with the immense flood of emotions that he feeling, there it stood. Before him and before he was ready to deal with it.

Butcher stood in front of the barn and as it appeared, the barn stood in front of him.

The moment approached him so quickly and he was engrossed in his own thoughts he found himself suddenly unprepared for the vision or for the reality of what was imminent.

CHAPTER TWENTY-FOUR

The White Knight

Rudi walked out of the house towards the barn. She was used to doing a quick clean up in the barn late at night. Not only did it make the next morning's chores easier but it was actually her favorite time to spend with the horses. It was quiet and dark and intense. Luke was away for the night on a short business trip. She trotted along the old path to the barn in her muck boots with the moon leading her way. The moon was full and bright white like the head of a lit flashlight. When the moon was full over the farm a bright light shown on the ground illuminating it like a flood light.

Rudi stopped to notice the moon and comment to herself how bright white and beautiful it was.

The air was warm and smelled of honeysuckle. She paused for a moment to take in the aroma. Rudi found solace and fulfillment with the horses, dogs and taking care of the plot of earth she felt responsible for. Nature was a precious rental. She did not feel ownership of her woods, barn and life that now thrived on the farm. She felt as if she was the caregiver who at this point in time and history was deemed worthy of nurturing it.

She opened the latches to the barn door. As she did Java called out to her. She laughed and walked over with the bucket of mints. As she opened the mints, Java heard the wrinkling of the cellophane and thrust his head over the bars of his stall. Java stood crunching his mint as Rudi walked through his stall. She thought of all the animals she had found, placed or was unaware of that lived in this spot and found it to be a comfort zone such as the young fawn. She moved out his stall exiting from the stall door that led to the next stall. This adjoining stall was empty. She moved through the empty stall opening the metal latch to Billy's stall that was on the end of the stall row. Billy was waiting his turn for a mint. She opened the mint and shoveled it into his mouth. She continued to walk through Billy's stall to turn right exiting through a small wooden stall door that lead to the center corridor and back supply room. Rudi grabbed a pick and retraced her steps back into Billy's stall, pushing the wheelbarrow as she made her way back to Billy's stall.

As the horses moved she could hear only the barn sounds, hay, horse's breath and the sound of small cracking and stretching from their stiff joints. She paused for a moment straining to hear a sound uncommon to the nightly movement of the horses. She heard it again. It sounded like the stones on the driveway announcing a visitor as they struck against one another under the pressure of the rubber tires. She knew it was not Luke. She put down the pick and left the stall to walk through the back wooden exit door and down the center corridor to look out of the window. She pressed her hands against the window and to her face to her hands. She saw a car out across the road. The neighbor's driveway was also covered with stone. "The car must have been a neighbor," she thought. She turned and walked back to the end stall to finish mucking it out. She noticed that clouds had cast out the clear moon and a steady rain was falling.

She finished the stall and moved the wheelbarrow to the stall door that separated Billy and the empty stall. As she pulled the metal spring lock open and the wheelbarrow slammed against the door shoving it back to the outer wall. She forced the wheelbarrow through the small entrance door and set it down. She paused at the sound of the front latch of the barn opening. This was unmistakable and she did not doubt her hearing this time. She stopped and held her breath. She filtered out the horse noise and stood frozen, not sure at this moment of what she should do until she determined who the intruder was. She stood still, breathed shallow, and heard nothing. Unable to move or even breath. "The sound was unmistakable, I did not imagine it," she said to herself. It was not Luke; she sensed something was terribly wrong. She felt strange, cold and scared. A feeling she is not accustomed too. She did not want to act impetuously but felt a keen sense of danger. Every nerve in her body alarmed her that this person intended harm. Java called out in a nervous whinny.

She decided to make a move toward the back of barn to exit from Billy's stall. "Once outside I see if there is a car in the driveway and run into the house." She slowly walked away from the wheelbarrow, back through the open metal adjoining stall door and back into Billy's stall. There she would turn right and exit through the large sliding door that flanked the back of Billy's stall and exit the barn into the woods. She walked into Billy's stall he did not move from his hay feeder. She slowly walked back to the sliding door to slide it open with her hands. It would not move. She tried again. "Fuck, it must be caught on something." Sometimes the door will not slide due to hay being stacked too closely to the track.

She stopped and heard movement down the center corridor. "Once the intruder gets to the end he or she will only be inches from where I stand," she thought frantically. She thought it strange that the intruder found the center corridor. The barn was dark; she did not turn on the lights. To find the center corridor you would have to enter the barn, turn right and turn left. There are two doors that must be opened. The barn was a maze of doors, turns and walk ways. The 115 year old structure housed many animals over the years and had the stalls divided many ways. "Who would know this?" she thought.

She turned and quickly moved back through the stall, ducking down as she crept through Billy's stall into the empty stall between Java and Billy. She paused to look through the open hay feeder that was accessed by the center corridor. The barn was very well planned out when the original farmers built it. Each stall was in a row along the lower part of the bank barn. A center walkway separated it from another row of stalls that ran along the side of the barn that was in the grounds. Each stall had a cut out and the walls slanted out to the corridor for easy feeding of hay. From the upper level of the barn, hay bales could be thrown down from a center door, ladder steps descended to the lower level and the hay could easily be disbursed to the various stalls by tossing the bales into the slanted hay feeders that were waist high.

Rudi leaned her back against the wall, tucked down she looked around the wall and through the hay feeder. She saw the back of a large male figure. Dressed in black walking down the corridor. He was steps from the end where he would have to turn and return down the path or turn left into Billy's stall or right into the storage room. She quickly ducked her head back as to not be seen if he turned to head back.

She was now filled with fear and panic. She quickly moved back to the middle of the stall and over to the metal stall door that adjoined the stall to Java's. The spring locks on the stall were rusty. It took effort to spring the latch back and the metal spring would sound a clanging noise once released. She attempted to open the latch but knew the noise could not be muffled. As she did, the figure also heard the metal spring and ran back down the corridor to the entrance of Java's stall. Rudi turned and jumped out through the hay feeder and into the center corridor. She heard the intruder fumbling with the latch of Java's stall door. The only entrance to the center stall where she stood was through Java or Billy's stall. She now stood in the center corridor. She was determined to escape. She climbed up the wood ladder that led to the upper hayloft. Once in the hayloft she would climb over the wall and out the small hidden door of the front of the barn that was built into the hillside. This would not be easy. The wall that surrounded the hayloft was 5 if not 6 feet high. Hay was stacked 20 to 30 feet high. The only light she had was the beams of light shining through the cracks of the wooden planked walls.

She reached the top of the stairs and pulled herself up to the hayloft. Rudi felt safer with the knowledge the she knew this barn inside and out. An intruder would not. She reached up and grabbed the top of the third row of hay that stood three feet tall and began to navigate up the steeping mountain of hay towards the wall. She placed her feet on the bales; she would sink into the cracks. Bales were stacked side by side but she would not see where one stopped and the next started. As she frantically climbed the bales, her left ankle slide down, her balance was lost and the left side of her body lowered three feet between the bales. Her entire left leg was trapped between the rows of hay. Her ankle was twisted in the hay. She struggled to release herself with her hands pushing upward on each side of the hay bales. Suddenly, one of the large front sliding doors of the upper barn pulled open. The large 25 foot door introduced the presence of the intruder. The moonlight flooded into the barn. Rudi was 10 feet above the stranger's vision and in clear view. She turned her body to see the oncoming stranger. Her weight shifted and the precariously stacked bales shifted with her. The top row of 30 bales leaned toward Rudi and tumbled to the ground like rocks falling from a cliff. Rudi fell to the ground with the falling hay. Once on the ground she was acutely aware that she only had seconds to lift her body off of the floor and flee back down the steps. She assumed the intruder would scale the wall to the hayloft that she had been frantically trying to reach.

Rudi rolled over to her knees and crawled the few feet to make it to the entrance of the ladder that would now descend her to the lower level of the barn. She slipped, missing the first two rungs and her hands slid down the ends of the old splintered wood. Her boot caught the next rung and she jumped off it onto the ground below. She ran back down the corridor and into Billy's stall. "This is not the safe stall, it is exposed at the end of the corridor," she told herself. "Go through it, into the empty stalls and crouch in the corner of Java's." There she would wait until it quieted down and then she would climb out Java's window and into the paddock. The intruder will waste enough time searching the hayloft for her. A stranger would not know the paths of the barns labyrinth. She felt confident as navigated the steps to ensure her survival.

She sprang the lock back without hesitating this time. She was running against the intruder now. Getting into position and remaining quiet was her main priority. As she crouched down moving into the back corner, Java shuffled nervously sensing her tension. She had not closed the door between his stall and the adjoining empty one. Rudi looked back and thought, "Java please do not push that open, stay in here, please. Quiet." She softly out to him. "Ssshhh, it's okay." She tried again to stifle him.

At that very second the door to the stalls slammed open. The old wood careening back off the side of the barn. She heard two steps up and onto the concrete floor.

Rudi was now shocked. "How does this person get down here so quickly? Actually, this person has navigated the paths and rooms of this barn all along. This person knows this barn!" Her mind detailing the steps she took and discovering that the stranger was always a step behind her on the same paths. "How could this be?"

She stopped to listen. Java turned and walked towards the front gate that opened up to where the stranger stood. She heard two more steps on the concrete. The sound of was a slow, organized large man.

Java did not move. He stood still, ears twitching to sounds. He instinctually stood motionless. The moon shown into the stall through the cracks of the barn but could not penetrate the corner where she crouched with her head in her hands. She could not contort her body to be any smaller.

There was silence again. She did not hear anything. "I cannot move, or breath, he is waiting for me to move," she said to herself with conviction and self control.

She looked up and saw the figure looking into the stall at the entrance to Java's stall. She could clearly see him but was unaware if he could see her in the shadow. He stood there without movement as a still frame. He looked almost unreal, like a mannequin. He was not moving, or speaking. Rudi was terrified of the silent strange actions of the man.

She looked down the outline of the large quiet figure. She could not see his face. He was wearing a black hooded sweatshirt and black jeans, black boots. He looked at his arms and followed the extremity down to his hand. He did not wear gloves. He had a gun in his right hand. Her eyes widened and filled with tears.

He stood still, motionless.

He reached his left hand into the pocket of his sweatshirt and pulled out a cell phone. Rudi watched on with confusion. "Is he calling someone else? Why, are there more?"

The man dialed a number and lifted the phone to his ear.

"It's me. You need to come here now. DON'T ask me any questions. Just get here now."

He disconnected the call and placed the phone back in his pocket. He opened the latch to the stall door. Java moved away from her and over into the moonlight flooding the stall through the open window. Java's eyes were wide and his nostrils flared. He was breathing hard and shifting his weight nervously now poised to flee. The door opened and man started to take a step in and stopped. He noticed Java. His copper red coat glistened in the moonlight. He moved toward the wall then moved back. Java's steps were short and quick. Java was trapped, Rudi was trapped.

The man stared at the horse. He stepped back. "You in the corner, stand up," Rudi did not obey. "Stand up!" he yelled. She did not. She could not.

"Noah?" said the man. Rudi was still crouched down in a tight small ball. She lifted her eyes up over her hands that cradled her face. She still did not speak. She could not break the silent barrier that kept her safe. "Noah?" the man said again. This time she could hear a sobbing tone to his voice. He was crying.

He turned to horse. "Coffee?" He took a step towards Java and said it again, "Coffee?" His voice denoted the conflicted emotions he was feeling. Java took a step towards the man. The shroud of fear left and he was not afraid of the intruder for some reason. Rudi figured out that it was the tone of his voice. The man was not loud or harsh. He was quiet. He was crying. Horses sense the tone, speed and aura of people. This man no longer frightened Java.

He held out his hand and stepped closer to Java. He touched his neck.

Rudi looked at the open stall door. She thought of dashing for the door while he was preoccupied with Java. As she moved the smallest muscle, her ankle cracked.

The man turned and stared at her.

He stepped backwards holding the gun out at her. He stepped back until her reached the ledge that bordered the exterior wall of the stall. He sat down to Rudi's surprise.

"Do you know? Do you know?" He said again louder.

At this point, Rudi felt the man losing grasp of the situation. She felt speaking would be in her best interest. "Know what?" she asked. She thought she would try to calm the man down and possible stop an impetus act performed out of his fluctuating emotions.

"This farm, this stall, this horse, where you are crouching." He spoke quietly with sadness. "I lived here. I grew up here. My brother died in this stall, with this horse, my horse, Coffee."

Rudi listened. She was astonished at the words. Noah? Coffee? The carvings in the wall were she crouched in the stall when Java almost died. NOA / Noah COFE/ coffee. It was making sense to her. The similarities? The stalls, the farm, the dreams, the horse's names, Coffee and Java.

As the man continued to speak, she thought that she recognized his voice. She listened trying to place it with a face. She looked into his face hidden by the shadow of the hood. She could recognize his features. He was just dark. She listened.

Peter told her the story. Of the horse, Coffee. Of his brother, Noah. Of the shooting, dismembering and burial. Most importantly, the plot contrived between his mother and father.

"My life stopped that night. Coffee and Noah had places in my life that could not be filled after that night." The man explained his emotions, fears and thoughts.

"Did you know this before you moved here? Before you took over this property and put horses in this stall?" he asked her. "No," she replied. "I moved here because it was in heart. It was in my soul. It was my destiny. I do not know you," she continued, "But you are not a lost soul. You were placed on this path that you can change. You did not kill me. You have not hurt this horse. You loved your brother." She was trying desperately to assuage him.

"Please let me go. I love this home, this horse, this property, don't you see that?" Peter did not answer her. He turned and walked out of the barn. Rudi did not move. She did not stand nor get up for fear that if she did, he would kill her.

Java did not flee the stall either. He stood by Rudi. Assessing the situation as she did, calculating flight.

It seemed hours later that she heard the stones on the long driveway move announcing the second intruder. She listened. The stranger had not spoken to her since leaving the barn.

She could not see the second man but heard their conversation.

The second man sounded older. He spoke with authority. "Is this his father?" Rudi asked herself.

"What the fucking hell are you doing Butcher?"

"Is she done?" Asked Aces.

"No, she is in the barn."

"WHAT, you brought me here and exposed me to this fed cunt witness?" Aces was angered.

"Fed Witness?" Rudi was straining to hear the conversation and assiduously scanning her mind for connection. "FEDS, this is the guy from Houston, the airport, the plane, the picture." It was all coming together for her. She recognized the man. The recognition and placement only astonished and frightened her more. The mindless collision of happenings. Fate bound and destiny determined.

"Look, I can't mother fucking do this. Do you understand? This is fucked up. I am done. I am fucking done. I am stopping. Fuck this. I made a decision, to fight. Twenty years ago. I now decide to forgive. Do you get me? Fight or forgive. I am fucking sick of fighting, Aces." Butcher was rambling almost incoherently. "Forgive this and end this, man." He repeated.

"Don't fucking say my name Butcher or I will shut you the fuck up!" Replied Aces, not yielding to Peter's emotions or evident breakdown. "What the fuck is wrong with you? What did you take?" he asked Peter.

"I loved you. I love you as my father. The rotten cunt bastard is dead and I looked at you as his replacement. Do this for me. Help me." He pleaded with Aces. "Let me out. I want out. I'm tired." Peter spoke with emotion unheard of within the biker gang. The word "Love" was taboo. He was not really a Skald within his soul and makeup. He was a SKALD through desperation. It was obvious that Aces was uncomfortable with the emoting tone and language.

"Tired of what? Me? The family that took you in and gives you income? You are a thankless prick!" Aces was not connecting with Peter's level of adulation for him.

"I want out! I am tired. I am done. If you ever cared about me let me out." Peter pleaded.

"Out of what?" Replied Aces.

"Out of this fucking hell that I am in. Three marks in one month? What the fuck do you think I am? I did not sign up for this, I am not your whore! I am nobodies whore, not yours, not nobodies." Peter was becoming impatient with Aces apathy and lack of accommodation.

"I want out. I ain't doin' this anymore, understand? I am not doin this mark. Not here, not now, not ever! Let it go. I'll accept the consequences."

"Don't be so fucking stupid!" Replied Aces. "You want some white knight title here? For what? Your old home? The fucked up cunt of a father that topped your little brother and family pet? The fucking mother that let it happen? You are willing to do time for them?"

"You are not understanding me. I will not do this; I will not let you do this. You were my father. If you ever felt love for me as a son you will honor my wishes." Peter was done. This was his last statement and Aces sensed it. Aces did love Peter. He did not have children. Children that he fathered or loved at least.

He looked at Peter. He looked into his dark, sad, hollow eyes. He sensed that he needed an act. An act of support. Maybe someone to stand up for him.

"If I allow this, you leave. You leave the group, do you understand?" Aces showed a weakening of emotion never displayed to Peter before.

"I understand the score Aces." Replied Peter.

"Leave, I will take of this." Replied Aces.

"NO. I do not want her topped Aces. It's over, here, now." Peter had nothing to lose and he was determined not to back down to Aces at this stage.

"You leave, I will follow and she goes unharmed. We both walk away."

"What if I don't Butcher?" Aces felt an internal inclination to show his authority as Peter was making all the requests.

"If you don't, I'll kill you." Peter held up the gun to Aces head. "I don't want to do that, but I will." He held the gun firm and high at Aces left temple.

Neither spoke for a seconds if not a minute. Aces knew the seriousness and Peter know the indelible act.

Aces turned and started to walk away. As he walked away he said to Peter, "I hope you know what you are doing my son."

Peter watched through tearful eyes as he mounted his bike and drove down the driveway.

Rudi was an impartial bystander in the fate of her life. She listened and believed in her heart that she was not brought to this place for death. The path she took, the path that was placed in front of her had to mean more than death. She looked up at Java. "This poor man, he is not a monster," she thought. She sensed that when they first spoke in the airport. She felt the same protective nature towards him that she felt towards the property, the animals and the horses. She was not the caregiver of Brown Hill Farm.

Peter walked back into the stall. He looked at Rudi and said, "This farm, these horses, the lives that live here matter." He turned and walked out of the barn.

Rudi sat in the corner silent. She knew that it mattered. When you do something in your life that is a sacrifice, a struggle, somewhere at sometime it matters. Peter knew his actions that night were not of Butcher's but of Peter's. They are not of Joe's but of a man who felt strength and courage and conviction. Actions of man who made a decision to quit running. The moment was awkward. Aces left. Peter was overwrought with emotion and Rudi was motionless. All life stopped for minutes or at least at the farm at that very moment in time.

CHAPTER TWENTY-FIVE

Corrections

She did not get up for what seemed other to be an hour or so. She feared that what she deciphered as her allowance for life would be false.

Once she felt the man would not return or change his mind she stood up. Numb and automated she closed the stall door and exited the barn latching the door as the security guard.

She slowly walked to the house. The air had cleared and the cloud moved. The moon was refulgent and high in the midnight sky. She did not know how long she had been in the barn. When she entered the house she went into the kitchen she walked to the desk in the corner. She pulled open her organizer drawer and pulled out her message pad. She calmly leafed through the pages until she found the name and telephone number of the Federal Agent that had called her the other day.

She put the numbers into the phone and held the phone to her ear. A voicemail message sounded as she expected,

"You have reached the voice mailbox of Agent Carderos. Please leave a message and I will return your call as soon as possible."

Rudi spoke slowly and without emotion.

"Mr. Carderos, this is Rudi Hudson. I received your message the other day regarding my cooperation with identifying the man on the Houston-Pittsburgh flight. I have been trying to jog my memory of the event and the man. I regret to inform you that I cannot remember his face. I do however, remember the face of the companion. Call me when you get this message."

She hung up the telephone and felt a calm peaceful rush come over her body. She thought the events and concluded that, "lives were taken decades ago but three lives were saved this night, whether it was Melinda or Rudi, Coffee or Java, Peter or Noah. History does not always repeat itself, sometimes it corrects itself."

She made the decision not to identify Peter. She would identify the other man unbeknownst to her. She walked over to the sofa and sat looking out to the moonlight night. She did not call Luke. Her thoughts were on the quiet tormented man with the dark eyes. She wondered if he would find his way to a new life now. She was drawn to him. He saved her life.

She did not consider that he was sent to take her life only that he saved it. She looked out at the woods imagining if he was still there.

She did not feel frightened or in danger. She felt she had a white light around her, protecting her. She sat staring out at the barn, the moon and the woods. She knew she would never see him again and that made her sad for some reason.

She felt lonely. She did not know why but she did. She sat there for a few more moments and made the conscious decision that she should call Luke.

She thought of Luke. How wonderful and kind and loving he was. "He was never mysterious or deep though," she said to herself. "Mysterious and deep is obviously a very dangerous thing," she was aware that she needed to be more realistic with the situation that had just occurred. "I need to call Luke and tell him," she said. She knew he would tell her to phone the police. How will she explain why she didn't? "Oh, I didn't call the police because I am trying to protect the quiet, yet deep stranger who came here to kill me and kept me hostage in my barn for hours while he struggled with the decision to shoot me?" She explained out loud in the dark room. "This is fucking crazy! What am I doing?"

She picked up the phone and dialed Luke's cell number.

"Hello?"

"Hello," she replied.

He knew immediately by her voice that something was wrong. Her voice did not project the dire events however. "What's up, are you okay?" he asked.

"Yes, no, I don't know. Something crazy happened tonight." She said calmly.

"Crazy as in the horses or crazy as in the house?" he asked.

"Crazy as in a stranger showed up while I was in the barn and he had a gun." She was telling him the events as if she saw them on television. She spoke about the scenario as if she did not live it.

"What? Are the police there? Were you hurt in any way?" he was now clearly frantic.

"No, I was not hurt."

"Rudi, I am coming home now. I am going to the airport. Stay on the phone and keep talking to me. Are the police still there?" he asked again.

"No, they are not here." She replied.

"Why the hell would they leave you there alone?" he asked with anger in his voice.

"Because, I did not call them." She replied with the full understanding that he was not going to comprehend her actions.

"What? "Why the hell not?" Luke was angry and confused.

"Can I tell the story when you come home? PLEASE? I am not in danger, it is a crazy story. I would prefer to tell you when you are here. I am okay, the horses are okay. It was just really scary and strange." She pleaded for him to acquiesce to her request.

"Rudi, I am not comfortable with this. What if he comes back?" he asked. He did not even know if it was a "he" or a "they".

"Please Luke. I am in the house. The doors are locked and I have the alarm on." She replied. She had done none of the actions she had told him that she did. She walked to the door as they spoke and locked it.

"I am going to go upstairs and lay down until you get here. Please call me when you land and when you get to the driveway so I do not freak out when I hear the stones." She asked of him.

"Rudi, I am leaving the hotel room now, I will be in the terminal in a few minutes." Luke had stayed at the hotel that as adjoined to the airport. "I love you honey. I will be home shortly. If you need me, or anything call me." He replied.

"I will be fine. I promise I am okay and I am not in danger. I love you too." She said to try and calm him down. She knew he would be upset. He was actually more upset than she was.

"Okay, I am going so I can make time. Call me, I love you." And with that he hung up. She could imagine him running through the airport. He was always there to rescue her ever since she met him.

She placed the phone back on the base. She poured herself a large glass of wine and shut off the lights as she walked upstairs to the bedroom. She admitted to herself that she must be in some state of shock. "I am not crazy, or crying, or scared..." she thought. "I am either losing my mind or I am in some post traumatic state."

She drank the wine while she lay in bed. It was hours before she fell asleep. Her mind spent the majority of the time on the stranger. As she felt the effect of the wine, her thoughts were becoming erratic and she knew she was falling asleep. She could no longer picture his face. He was just a dark figure. The dark figure faded and she slept.

CHAPTER TWENTY-SIX

Like Father

Butcher left the barn and headed down the driveway toward the front road to be sure that Aces had actually left the property. He did not want to refute Aces words but he was felt chosen to become the protector at this given juncture to Rudi, the farm and the horse.

Aces had clearly left the property. Peter quickly turned and headed through the woods, back toward the meeting spot. He ran as quickly as he could. With every footstep pounding the wet path he feared that Dempsey left the spot and witnessed the agreement between he and Aces. Dempsey was the only instrument in the equation that could change the dynamics. Peter was acutely aware that Dempsey would not risk going to jail for anyone, not even his own mother. He and Peter never bonded although they worked closely together. "If Dempsey has a chance to bring me down before him he will not hesitate." He told himself as the meeting spot drew closer as he continued to run.

He thought of the woman running through the barn like a small scared field mouse. He thought that was how Noah must have felt the night he died. He was nauseated with the thought of the level of fear the woman and Noah must have reached.

He smiled as he thought of his actions tonight. He was proud of himself for the first time in a lifetime. It was a euphoric rush that made him feel unlike any drug he had consumed. He reached the spot and could see Dempsey off about 20 feet sitting in the truck with the window open smoking.

As he knelt in the woods Dempsey opened the truck door and looked around. Peter held his breath and restricted every muscle from moving. He could not risk being seen. He would not be able to explain why he was hiding and where the girl was.

Dempsey walked around to the back of the truck and was new leaning against the tailgate. He looked at his watch and mumbled something. He regained his balance and looked around him.

Peter took a moment to contain his composure and to calculate his next steps. His plan was to remove the threat of Dempsey finding out that the mark still lived. Peter reached around and removed the backpack from his back. He grabbed the gun and placed it into his pants. He removed other items and left the bag off to the side.

Dempsey flicked his cigarette but to the ground. He stood up and took about 5 steps towards the woods. His ears strained to hear movement. He thought her heard the snapping of dry brittle sticks left on the ground from last autumn.

As he turned in a 360 panoramic movement he turned to the large dark looming vision of Peter standing a foot away. "How did I miss him coming up on me?" he said to himself once the startling appearance translated to "Peter?"

Peter did not say a word and Dempsey did not have a chance to either. Peter lifted the axe overtop of his head and swung it downward onto Dempsey's foot. The finely honed blade of the axe that was meant to dismember the girl sliced through Dempsey's boot and removed all five of his toes. Dempsey buckled over grabbing at his amputated toes. He fell to his knee and without hesitation Peter lifted the axe and swung it harder with even more conviction over his head and down onto

Dempsey's remaining foot chopping his remaining toes off from his foot. Dempsey fell onto his back and rolled over in a fetal position. He was screaming in agonizing pain as Peter kicked his side.

"Mother fucker, you cunt bastard!" he was screamed at him.

"You're right fucker, I am just like my old man." Peter had an uncontrollable amount of unbridled strength and adrenaline rushing through his body. Every ounce of rage that ever filled his psyche was directed at Dempsey.

"What the fuck are you doing?" Dempsey screamed back at him. He tried to stand but could not. He rolled over to the truck and tried to grab the wheel for balance. He managed to get to his knees and grab the top of the metal that formed the bed of the pickup truck. The large strong man struggled to gain any balance or control over his frame.

He fell back down. Peter laughed at him. "Without toes you fucker you cannot stand." He said in a cold, calculated calm voice. He regained control of his rage. Peter's largest asset to the gang was his strength but more so his ability to control his rage and strength to keep his head together. He stepped back and threw the axe off into the nearby brush.

Dempsey rolled to his knees again like a fly without wings he reeled desperately trying to find balance or stability.

"That's it, get on your knees you fucker." He kicked Dempsey from the side pushing him back over.

He stopped and allowed the moment without speaking again until Dempsey could comprehend was he was about to say.

The woods fell silent again. Dempsey was sobbing in pain, but very inaudibly.

Peter's voice was loud, strong and direct. "This is your last night on this earth Dempsey. In about 5 fucking minutes I am gonna fucking cut your arms, legs, hands, feet and fingers from your torso. But before I do that, you are going to fucking hear me out."

Dempsey looked up at Peter. He knew Peter was capable and serious. He began to crawl frantically to the cab of the truck. There he left his gun on the seat while waiting for Peter. He knew he was the one that now fucked up by leaving it behind.

Peter hung back, watching and reveling in Dempsey's actions. He knew he had the power now. He permitted Dempsey to make it to as far as the door. As Dempsey struggled once again to get off of the ground using the stumps left on his feet, he struggled. Peter kicked him away with a hard blow to his side. This time while he was down, Peter kicked him onto his back and immediately without hesitation, drove the heel of his boot into Dempsey's nose dislodging his septum. He kicked his face so hard that his nose was no longer recognizable as the center focus of his face. It was smattered to his face with a gush of blood running down his face, chin and into his mouth. Dempsey started choking and spitting from the tremendous flow of blood now pouring down the back of his throat.

"Do you think I am fucking STUPID? YOU MUST! You have been calling me a stupid cunt for seven years now." He asked him as he reached for what used to be his nose.

"Am I a stupid cunt now or are you?" He again questioned Dempsey.

"This is fun but we need to move on fucker. Look at me." He moved over and stood large in front of Dempsey on the ground.

Dempsey did not look up. "You fucking pussy, quit fucking moaning and look at me!" He placed the bloody heel of his boot onto his chest restricting Dempsey from moving or rolling away from focusing on him.

"We have been brothers for seven years now. You have kicked me down every day. I am curious Dempsey. Why do you think you are better than me?" he asked him again, "seriously, what made you better than me?"

Dempsey looked at him and said, "Because I am. You are a farmer's son. You are the son of a butcher and murderer of his own flesh and blood. But you Butcher, are the son of a liar and the bastard of a lying whore of a take it up the ass mother."

Peter did not respond as most men would, with impulsive reaction. He reached into his pants and pulled the gun out. He placed it in front of Dempsey's face. "See this Dempsey. If I am the stupid one, why am I standing over you about to blow your balls off?"

"You were placed in the Skalds at number two not because of your fucking brains but because of your fucking old man. I made it where it did because of me. My old man did not open any fucking doors but you know what Dempsey, it made me stronger than you."

"You have some fucked up false sense of brains and strength. It's just that, false."

"I am the son of Joe Bauchmann and son of Melinda Bauchmann and the brother to Noah Bauchmann," he spoke with reverence for the first time since that indelible night.

This was the first time he spoke their names out loud.

"You are the son of a drunken gambler who took advantage of other people's misfortune. You are the son of a woman whom you never met. And you are brother to no one. Not even the 200 brother's in this gang. "We all hated your fucking guts, you maggot."

With that end, he raised the gun up to Dempsey's head and took one shot that pierced through the front temple of his bloodied face. Dempsey's head and neck fell limp to the side and his body followed.

Butcher turned and walked to the back of the truck.

He took out the tarp and carried it over to where the body of Dempsey lay. He opened it up beside him and kicked his body onto it with his feet. He went into the truck and removed his gun and cell phone, picking up both items with the bottom of his shirt.

He threw the items on the tarp beside Dempsey's body.

Peter then walked over to the brush and pushed it to the side looking for the axe. He saw it and picked it up and headed over to where the backpack laid on the ground. He looked for it and once spotted picked it up.

He removed only Dempsey's head, feet and hands. He placed his severed body parts into a plastic bag as requested by Aces of the mark. He threw all of Dempsey's personal items onto the tarp and rolled it up. He walked to the back of the truck and opened the tailgate. He grabbed twine and tied up each end of the tarp and the center. He laughed at the analogy he had, it looked like a tied piece of meat that his mother would get from the butcher.

He jumped up onto the truck bed and dragged the body up onto the bed.

Once up and onto the back of the truck, Peter carried out the same plans that had been detailed and plotted by Dempsey. The same path, hole and method meant to dispose of the mark.

Peter opened the door to the truck and turned the keys. The radio was on and the words to Pink Floyd's 'The Wall' were filling the silence of the cab.

Peter drove quietly and slowly through the back roads used by the gas company to navigate the gas pipelines. He drove for approximately 10 minutes. He arrived at the spot where the truck was to be left. The next quarter of a mile or so would have to be done by foot. Dempsey and Butcher were meant to carry the girl, bury her, Dempsey would go to where his bike was hidden, and the same for Butcher.

Peter got out and walked around to the back where he dragged Dempsey's body off and slung it over his shoulder. He found the strength to carry the body all the way to the dumping site. The hole was already dug by Dempsey earlier that evening. "The miserable fuck dug his own grave." Peter said aloud softly. As navigated the path her heard Dempsey's cell phone ring again. He laughed and commented aloud, "Dempsey isn't here anymore."

He threw the body in and began shoveling the soil and clay onto of him. Once finished he stomped the ground down and drug branched and brush over. He covered the ground with the natural ground cover of the woods and headed back to the truck.

Once he got there he took the bag containing Dempsey's head, hands and feet with him. He walked back through the quiet damp woods. The moon glowed brightly in the dark night sky assisting him with navigating the narrow paths.

He was close to concluding this chapter of his life. Violence had consumed the majority of his life. He planned to get on his bike and ride away from it all. He thought if he could leave the physical boundaries the contained the space and time where the violence occurred, he would be freed from it.

He reached his bike and tied the garbage bag to the back rack with bungee cords. He pushed his bike down the path towards the road. Once on the road he continued to push the bike. He had no concept of time or how long it had taken him once he returned to the spot to meet Dempsey.

As he pushed his bike on the side of the road, headlights shown in front of him from an approaching truck. His instincts heightened and he felt a rush of adrenaline and fear. He had come too far to have another witness or even worse, the cops. He quickly straddled his bike and started it. "I can't have someone think I broken down." He thought to himself. The bike started and he drove slowly on.

The vehicle illuminating the dark desolate road stayed steadily and even paced behind him. He did not turn nor act suspicious. He looked in the rear view mirror. It was Aces pickup truck.

He pulled over and turned off his bike. Aces drove up beside him and shut off the truck.

"Where is Dempsey?" he called out from the far window of the front seat.

"I don't fucking know Aces. I have my own agenda at the moment." He pulled a cigarette from his leather jacket pocket and lit the needed instrument meant to calm his nerves. "Why, am I supposed to be his keeper now?" He asked with an intended air of focus and control.

"Cut the shit Butcher. He was supposed to meet me at his bike after this fucking plan went tits up. I tried to call him but his phone rang off. When did you last see or talk to him?" Aces was direct and showed diminishing patience toward Peter's conduct.

"I went back to the meeting spot and told him that he had to speak with you about the mark. Where or what the fuck he did after that is not my concern Aces. I have enough on my mind right now."

He did give me a bag with the shit from the job in it. I'm gonna put it in the back of your truck." Peter was not asking for authorization but pronouncing that he was putting Dempsey's tools in his truck for Aces to deal with.

He got off of his bike and moving hastily he walked around to the back of his bike and untilled the garbage bag. He removed the bag that contained Dempsey's severed head, hands and what was left of his feet, and placed the bag in the back of Aces pickup truck with care. The black garbage bag was tied but he did not want the dismembered head to roll around fearing it would stir a reaction from Aces.

After he placed the bag in the bed of the truck he walked back over the passenger window.

"I'm off." He turned and mounted his bike. Aces drove off and Peter watched as his car faded away around the last bend of the desolate foggy road.

He started his bike and drove in the opposite direction. For the first time in over two decades he felt free. He felt a sense of control over his life. The objects on the road that appeared to him through the fog became clear. As he navigated the winding road his mind, his life, objects in front of him were coming into focus, yet his mind was determined to drift back to the woman at Brown Hill Farm.

"The strange frightened woman who saved my life tonight."

CHAPTER TWENTY-SEVEN

Presence Of Protection

Days after the indelible night in the barn, Rudi struggled to move on with her life. The farm, barn and property remained unsettled. She could not find satisfaction to the onslaught of questions she now had. She wanted to know about Peter, his life, Noah and the trouble that caused such wayward paths in this one man's life. She thought of contacting the realtor to forward her the name of the one child who sold the property to them.

"Bonnie," I think her name was. Rudi spoke to herself as she was slowly awaking from an ungratified night of sleep. Luke had already dressed and left for work. He was working more hours and traveling more trying to get established in his new territory. This left Rudi with endless amounts of time to think and communicate with herself. "Okay, I will get up and go riding this morning. I have not ridden in a week." She said to herself in an attempt to motivate herself. She got out of bed and got dressed to go riding.

Rudi entered the barn holding a cup of coffee and two carrots. Java and Billy looked up with wide eyes happy to see her. She looked back with warm eyes uplifted to see them. "Java Java we are going riding." She called out him. She walked over and gave him the carrot. He stole it from her hand. She walked over to Billy and handed him the second carrot. She rubbed his forehead and kissed his nose. Rudi loved the smell of the horses.

Every time she kissed them on the nose she thought of the smell of brewed English Breakfast tea. She reached over again and kissed him another time. The moment was quiet, satisfying and loving. She was decidedly happy that she got up to go riding. She walked back through the damp, dimly lit corridor toward the tack room. She picked up her saddle, reins, saddle pad and helmet. She struggled to carry all the necessary items into Java's stall. She flung the saddle over the stall door and walked in to saddle him up. As she slipped the reins over his head she looked out into the pasture. She noticed a female deer with two other doe's grazing. She stopped to give notice to the beautiful wildlife. She looked up at the trees spotted with black crows. Their loud cries beckoning to the others to come for left over sweet feed from the horses manure. This morning all events seemed right.

She paused while in Java's stall to glance over at the corner where she attempted to hide from Peter. She kept the mood positive as she saddled Java by hoping he moved on with his life. She had an unadulterated feeling of his safety. She thought of Peter often in any given day since the event in the barn that night. She felt connected to him. Her feelings started the day she met him at the airport and only intensified the night he saved her life.

There was a calming sense of safety and belonging to her life when she thought of Peter. She sensed his presence in this world although she did not know where he was. That was enough to constitute a relationship to her. The knowingness that he lived, somewhere, and was content, became an important part of her life. She hoped he thought of her. She was not presumptuous enough to say he did. She spent countless unmonitored seconds imagining him and his actions and movements at the same moment in time that she was thinking of him. She wondered if her thoughts of him transcended in the moment.

Before Rudi realized the time, Java was saddled and she moved her thoughts back to her task at hand. She had a conversation with the Federal Agent the day before. She recounted the conversation.

"I can recall the face of the one companion but I cannot remember the other." She said to the agent.

Rudi changed the players. She altered her version to recount the second man as the one who dropped the picture and Peter the man who accompanied him. She had an appointment to meet with a sketch artist at the federal building in Pittsburgh the next Monday. She tried to recall the second companions face although it was clouded by the visual memory of Peter's. She was determined to pay honor to him by attempting to keep him as safe as she could.

Rudi lead Java out of the barn. She walked him out and up the path while opening the large gate that lead back to the woods. She allowed the door to fall open as the large muscular chestnut horse walked through. He stopped and she shoved her left boot into the stirrup. She passed her right leg up and over his back to rest in the right stirrup. She picked up the reins and clicked her lips together twice. Java's ears perked up and he stepped forward high with a proud trot. Rudi's frame was petite but she had a great presence while riding. She sat tall in the saddle with perfect posture. Her black knee length riding boots pronounced her long muscular legs. Her chin lifted above her horses ears. Java moved with balance and motion. He had a great desire to please Rudi. He was calm and obedient. As they trotted up the path the leave began to swirl downward in front of the path. The sound of his metal shoes scraped the stones on the path. Each stick, leaf or undefined sound perked Java's ears and snapped him to attention. Java was like all thoroughbreds, high strung. As they reached the thick of the woods it was Rudi and not

Java that sensed a presence. She looked around but did not see anyone. The wind blew softly and the leaves swirled downward. One rested on the saddle. She brushed it off and pulled Java's reins back signaling for him to stop. He did. They both looked around, breathing softly as to not intrude upon the sounds. The "out of place" sound that they were both straining to hear. Rudi often paid notice to how acute her sense of hearing became when she rode. Since riding Java she opened her sense of sound to hear quite anonymous sounds that normally go unnoticed.

The air was still and the atmosphere was even more still. Java breathed out hard from his nostrils. This was a sign to Rudi that something was in the area, an animal usually. She calmly and softly kicked his sides with her boots. He walked on. As he moved past the area where they stood, she noticed smoke. She noticed a faint swirl of grey smoke through the dense trees. She did not panic. She did not feel any harm. The actor did not see her. She kept Java walking down the path. She stopped him once into the thick trees. She dismounted him and tied the reins around a tree. Java reached down to grab at the greens left of the forest floor. Rudi crept through the woods back around to where she saw the smoke. She came behind the trees, brush and back of a man. She crouched down behind a grouping of small trees. The man was distinguishable to her. It was Peter. Her heart jumped and her pulse fled. "Do I leave or approach him?" she asked herself. She did not speak to herself a second time. She moved forward without fear or camouflage. Peter turned quickly with sharp instinct. He looked at her with intense surprise and shock.

Rudi spoke up first. "We meet again." She said. He looked at her and flicked his cigarette to the ground, agitating his boot over the smoking end. He looked at her and spoke quietly and calmly, "You have a lot of balls lady."

"I do," She replied. She smiled easing the tense air. Peter was attempting to portray his demeanor as harsh but allowed his muscles to relax. It showed through his large shoulders. The easing was noticeable.

"What are you doing here?" she asked him.

"I am waiting." He replied.

"Waiting for what?" asked Rudi.

"Waiting to make sure you are okay."

She felt her eyes fill with emotion. "You don't need to continue protecting me." She said to him softly with heart.

"I do." He said.

"Are you okay? Will you be okay?" she asked him as she stepped even closer to the large imposing man who invaded her thoughts.

"Yes. I will be." He replied. They stopped speaking for a second. Or it may have been two. "Will I ever see you again?" Rudi asked him out of no instigation. Peter did not reply immediately.

"I am going to another state when I leave tonight." He told her. She did not understand the reason for her feelings but she felt sad and alone when she heard the words.

"Where will you go?" she asked him. His lips curved over his hardened face forming a slight smile.

"I can't tell you that."

"I know you did not ID me." He continued to say. "Thank you for this chance. You will be okay now. I promise."

Rudi did not ask him what he meant. She understood that he was referring to the fact that she did not identify him to the FBI. "I want you to be okay. I also need to thank you for saving me."

She suddenly felt his tension again. The mood had changed and it was time to leave. She was not ready for the moment that they were sharing to end. She wanted to embrace him. She had a need to physically feel his presence. She moved toward him. He did not step towards nor away from her. He stood firm without moving yet he allowed her to remove the distance he placed between them; the space of a mere 4 feet that embodied his sense of security.

"I will never forget you nor will I ever stop thinking about you," she said as she moved close enough to hug him. Peter instinctually raised his arms and held her close. His face rested on her head. He could smell her. She smelled of freshness. He breathed in while embracing her small frame.

They pulled away after a moment. They were both emotionally moved, happy, yet sorrow demanded its presence.

She turned and ran back through the woods toward Java. She was crying. She could not stop her tears. Was it for the loss, or was it for the tacit, redolent bound that transcended logic and reality of their two spirits? Although neither would share the same space in the same time again, each of them would always draw strength from their instinctual knowledge that wherever and whenever, they were thought of and cared for.

Rudi met up with Java. He turned his head as he heard her approaching. She stood by him allowing herself to show the emotions that she was feeling. Java sensed her mood and stood still. As she mounted him and turned him back toward the path she did not want to look back but could not avoid the need to know if he was really gone. She turned and he was. She knew he would be gone and that she would never see him again.

Rudi said to herself with proud proclamation, "I will take care of your home. It will flourish now that this burden has been lifted." Her tears fell onto the black leather saddle as the two rode, then trotted, then cantered down the path back towards Brown Hill Farm.

Rudi thought about the sedition that had played out in the last year since moving to the farm. "The farm chose me." She thought as she was intensely working out a higher purpose for the recent events. "I moved here expecting a change in my life and never expected to find such a purpose for my presence here."

As she reached the barn she took Java straight into his stall. She did not dismount him at the gate as normal. As she stood up and stretched her legs she looked around at the aged wood that commanded respect from a new vantage point.

"The reason for all of this," she thought, "Was to restore another's purpose in life and in turn equally make mine richer; by giving me the knowledge that I had a purpose." She smiled at Java and corrected herself, "have a purpose."

Would you like to see your manuscript become a book?

If you are interested in becoming a PublishAmerica author, please submit your manuscript for possible publication to us at:

mybook@publishamerica.com

You may also mail in your manuscript to:

**PublishAmerica
PO Box 151
Frederick, MD 21705**

www.publishamerica.com

CPSIA information can be obtained at www.ICGtesting.com
Printed in the USA
BVOW03s1730120114

341554BV00001B/64/P